A Dangerous Liaison

Phoenix Rising

By

Leslie LeBlanc

In loving memory of my grandmother, Freda Mildred Carey, who passed away during the writing of this story. The woman who gave me my first Harlequin that helped hook me on romance, and I've enjoyed reading the genre ever since. She will be missed.
I want to thank my husband Paul for his continued support, as well as my friend James for challenging me to better myself in my writing career as well as life in general. Sorry for being such a difficult student - Cheers.

Chapter One

Cassidy

"The food is wonderful. You've done an amazing job putting this together." Sheila, a counselor and former coworker of her mothers'.

The young-looking woman with chestnut hair and bright violet eyes offered a sympathetic smile and a hug, before scarfing down the last morsel of her piece of cake with a moan of satisfaction.

"Thanks, Sheila. It was nice of you to come."

They made their way to the kitchen table topped with trays of food, and drinks. The radio played softly on the counter. Faded, by Alan Walker. Losing her mother was hard enough without fighting memories of Chase. He was dead, gone, and nothing would bring him back.

Muffled voices carried from other rooms, coworkers of her mother, neighbors, not a large crowd, none were friends of hers. She rubbed over the stitches on her arm. Twelve of them. If only it were possible to forget.

She'd lost so much blood that night, roughly two weeks ago, but by some miracle she survived. That nightmare would never get erased. For several nights she lay in bed, staring at the ceiling in the dark, wishing she had died that night. Seeing the news, a constant bombardment, reminded her incessantly of the loss of her friends, her mother, everyone.

Nevermind having to attend three funerals while planning one. Marc and Stacy were her two best friends, and Jim, her old boss. She never heard of anything for Chase and assumed it due to military secrecy.

What did she really expect? Nobody realized how intimately involved they were, save for possibly Sergeant Major Mercer. There would be no folded flag showing up at her door, and no way to repair her broken heart. Two nights ago, she nearly gave up, on everything.

She'd reached into her nightstand, took her tactical knife, and heaved a heavy sigh. Placing the blade near her wrists she counted. One… Deep breath… Two… Another breath… A knock on the door.

In a slow saunter she crept downstairs, opened it, shocked to see her brother.

"Cassidy, are you alright?" Sheila stole her from those thoughts.

"I'm fine." She took a bite from a frosted piece of chocolate cake on the table.

She hadn't eaten in days and her stomach protested its emptiness.

"You sure?" Before she could give a reply, Joseph, her brother, approached.

They looked very similar, only he was about six feet tall, with an angular nose like their father, and their mothers' marble green eyes. She caught the warning eye Sheila gave him. He approached, hugged her as he did when he first arrived.

"Thank you again for taking me in. I understand it's not easy for you to take on an extra burden. Like I said, after hearing that I nearly lost you too... I don't want to live like that anymore."

"I'm glad to have you back, Joe, I really am." Her nickname for him since childhood.

She wrapped her arms around his gaunt frame. It was clear, another few months in that lifestyle and she'd have lost her brother for good.

"Tonight, we're going dancing. You've been through so much and we want to take care of you, at least for a night." Sheila placed a gentle hand on her shoulder as she released her brother, squeezing lightly.

She didn't want to go anywhere, do anything, she just wanted to die. Joe seemed to read her thoughts.

"Please, Cassy! We're all here for you, you shouldn't be alone. We'll get through this together." He understood her state of mind the moment she answered the door, the knife never left her hand until he pried it from her.

For hours he'd held her as she screamed and cried until keeping her eyes open became impossible.

"Yeah, please Cassy! We want to make sure you're OK and it's my medical opinion you really shouldn't be alone for a while." Sheila and Joseph exchanged knowing glances.

She had no desire to fight, argue, or discuss her pain.

"I'll buy you a couple of drinks." Sheila glared daggers at her brother.

"Are you sure that's wise?" She hissed.

"I can manage myself." Cassidy retorted defiantly at Sheila's disagreement.

"Alright, suit yourself." Sheila raised her arms in defeat.

Cassidy took another bite of cake.

"So you'll come?" Joseph seemed both surprised and pleased at the idea.

"Yeah, I could use a drink or two." *Or twelve...*

If they insisted on taking turns on suicide watch, she may as well try drinking herself into a stupor. Hopefully enough to forget everything. If she were to be honest, it would be so easy to fall right back into her old habits, drown in the same kind of lifestyle her brother later found himself in, things she hadn't told Chase.

"That's great!" Her brother exclaimed as he and Sheila hugged her simultaneously.

The phone in her purse went off, startling her. Hesitantly, she took it out, peered at the screen. Sergeant Major Mercer. He'd payed her in full, she'd finished her assignment, but he still insisted on calling over and over again. She tossed it back in her purse, smoothing the knee length silky black dress before running her fingers through her long honey-blond tresses. She'd avoid him until hell froze over. Didn't need another reminder of that painful ordeal.

"Who's that?" Joseph - Joe, asked.

"Nothing to worry about." There was no changing the subject fast enough. "We need to discuss moms' Will. You have to contact the lawyer before you can get what she left you."

No mistaking his lack of interest.

"Why bother? She probably didn't leave me anything because... You know. She and I haven't been close since then." His lifestyle made him a danger to himself and wore on mothers' heart, but she still loved him enough to leave him three hundred thousand dollars and her cabin by the lake.

Cassidy was her beneficiary on the insurance and received two million dollars, the vehicles, and the house. Too bad money couldn't replace people, otherwise, it might actually make her happy. Something she wasn't going to tell Joe. Didn't need the jealousy on top of everything else.

"She did, and I think you'll be happy, but you won't get it if you don't see the lawyer."

"OK, OK! I'll give him a call, tomorrow." She offered a hint of a smile.

"Thank you."

Until eight o'clock that evening she entertained guests, trying not to cry. It was the same as each of the funerals she attended. The shifty eyes, pointing and whispers, many two-faced people who offered condolences to her face while muttering about the possible state of her mental health when they didn't know she heard.

When the crowd left, the only remaining people were Joe and Sheila.

"You should change into something a little less depressing while we wait for a couple of people." Hard to believe Sheila was only thirty-six, a couple of years older than her, since the woman could easily pass for twenty.

With fine features and a slender form, she could turn heads with ease.

"OK..." She still lacked the desire to go along with this, but knew they wouldn't take 'no' for an answer, especially after seeing just how much time Sheila and Joe spent talking to each other.

Twenty minutes later she wore a sleeveless black cocktail dress, shimmering earrings beneath loose hair cascading below her shoulders, makeup meticulously applied, complete with smoky eyes and coral lips. She reached the bottom of the stairs as the doorbell rang.

"Great, they're here!"

Two women close to the same age as them. One had to be Sheila's sister because they looked identical. The other had long raven hair braided behind her back with eyes nearly dark enough to match. About the same height as Cassidy with shimmering high heels and a sleek short silver skirt and halter. Even her makeup appeared professionally done.

"Hey guys! I want you to meet Cassidy. I worked with her mother." They greeted her nonchalantly.

"Hey." She replied with equal vigor.

"Cassidy, this is is my twin, Annita, and my besty, Zoey."

"Nice to meet you." She forced a smile, wanting to get this over with.

"Let's go! Let's go!" Joe, impatient as always.

They hopped in a waiting cab, Zoey instructed the driver to take them to the Pearl Ultra nightclub.

Cassidy gaped, shocked.

"We got VIP tonight." Sheila winked.

That required a reservation! Cassidy's eyes widened. Was she really that predictable? Sheila chuckled at the look on her face.

"Don't worry about it. If not you, it would have been someone else. Glad it's you though. Nobody should have to deal with the things you have."

"Don't remind me." She muttered, crossing her arms.

"Right, sorry."

If they only knew the depth of her misery. They learned about her mother, her best friends, but not Jim or Chase, only because she never told Joe. She suspected he'd talked to Sheila before showing up the other night, based on how they interacted throughout the day, and the fact she seemed to know only the things told to him. Cassidy preferred it that way. Her life was her business. The less knowledge people had of her, the better.

The place looked packed, dark, save for strobe lights. At the center of the dance floor hung a massive mirrored ball. Smoke machines were at work, filling the air as the DJ played a familiar song she longed to ignore. Nobody would tell her not to have a broken heart in the club. She wondered if the person who wrote the song still would have had they been through the same. Doubtful.

Joe leaned in.

"What do you want to drink?"

"I don't care, but if it's hard make it a double." He nodded, headed to the bar.

"This way." Sheila led them to the couch in the VIP section after giving their tickets to the employee and receiving a stamp on their hands.

Sheila, Annita, and Zoey talked among themselves as she scanned her surroundings. The place was incredible, and busy. She wasn't one for crowds, content to just sit and people watch. Ironic considering she used to do security for concerts, not just office buildings. Joe returned with a bottle of Patron Silver and five shot glasses. She'd gone there once or twice before with Stacy. Bottles of liquor were not cheap.

"Here you go." He poured hers first, handed it over.

With a tilt of her head it burned its way down to her stomach. She slid it back as he poured the other four.

"Another." He obliged.

The women watched her warily. She hated being the center of attention.

"Don't push it Cassy, you've barely eaten in days. You'll make yourself sick." She glared at Sheila before slamming back another shot.

"I'll be fine. One more."

The way Joe and Sheila shot each other glances had her biting her tongue from asking what was between them.

"One more all around, then dance." Zoey suggested.

Aside from Cassidy, the decision was unanimous. As they headed to the floor she managed to sneak in one more shot. She reached the group about the time Iggy started singing about her team.

Tequila, being a slow acting poison, left her head swimming and body numb halfway through the song as they danced, packed tight like sardines. Her cares slowly melted away as the alcohol worked its magic. Her phone went off in her purse again and she checked. Mercer. The man didn't know when to give up. She threw it back in her purse. Perhaps a number change was a good idea.

When the song finished she returned to the couch, pouring another shot. She didn't care if she killed her liver. It was her fault that her best friends, Jim, and Chase were all gone. If not for her, they'd still be alive. Two more down before her brother and Sheila dragged her back to the dance floor.

Another few songs and her mind checked out, body on autopilot. She cursed when some guy approached. Attractive, but as bright as a burned out light bulb.

"Hey sugar." He greeted before grinding on her.

It took more effort than it should have to keep her temper in check.

"Sorry bud, not interested." Her words came out slurred.

She tried to move away, but he continued.

"You look like you've had a rough night and need a release. Lucky for you, I'm just the man for the job." He ran his fingers over her side, the same as Chase the day they played Truth or Dare at Mercer's safe-house, and his foot almost a lifetime ago.

A lump formed in her throat. Her stomach knotted and nausea threatened as a lifetime of memories overwhelmed her. Nobody could make her feel the way

Chase had, and no one had the right to try.

"Get your hands off me before I break them off!" She shoved him away, stumbling backwards, but the jerk acted as though he'd never tasted rejection before.

Joe stepped in, shoving the guy back before he was able to put another hand on her.

"She's not interested, so beat it!"

The man swore a long streak.

"Bitch is nothing but a tease anyway." He growled, marching off.

"You alright?" Joe asked, Sheila and her friends watched in stunned silence.

"I'm fine." She managed, visibly shaken. "I need some air."

They joined her outside but the fresh June night air didn't help, and the tequila reached its full strength, had her seeing double. Her phone rang again. Ripping it from her purse, she growled. Not again! Mercer was a stubborn man but there remained nothing to discuss. After a moment of temptation to just smash the annoying contraption she shut the power off and threw it back in her purse.

"Someone bothering you?"

"No, Joe, it's fine. Nothing to worry about."

"Wow, your friend's got more issues than a newsstand."

Cassidy glared, eyes shooting daggers of ice at Zoey.

"Leave her alone, she's been through a lot." Sheila shot back, clearly surprised at her friends lack of sense.

"I'd like to see you lose everything I did, see how well you do!"

Obviously, coming along had been a mistake.

"Hey, Zoey!" Annita interjected. "That was uncalled for." Zoey sighed, pulling a cigarette from the pack in her purse.

"Sorry, it's just hard to watch." As she spoke she lit it, inhaled deeply, exhaled slowly. "This is because of her psycho ex, right?"

Way to rub salt in the wound. After police found her number several times on his phone, they'd questioned her thoroughly before demanding she testify against him. They even retrieved copies of the text messages. Just one more thing to drive her crazy. With any luck he'd get euthanized.

"Piss off! That's none of your business." She muttered, in no mood to endure anymore crap.

"Well look who it is!" A statuesque man approached, flanked by menacing charcoal haired men who looked to be more brawn than brain.

They stood in stark contrast to his blond hair, blue eyes, and toned physique. Alarms sounded in her head. Something about him seemed eerily familiar, but she never met him before. The blond approached her, ignoring her entourage. Instinctively she backed away.

"Who the hell are you?"

"You don't need to worry about that. In fact, after tonight, you won't have to worry about anything ever again."

He took a gun from his side, aimed at her head. She was far too drunk to deal with this, dizzy, slow, and seeing double. It seemed futile to try to fight, but she did so anyway, wishing she had brought her gun, though knowing the club would never have let her in if she had.

Sheila and her company screamed bloody murder while Joe tried to help. In the end she wound up on her back, pinned down, immobile by the unknown assailant. The other two men became preoccupied with pounding and bloodying her brother and keeping the women from running for help. If she'd just kept sober, this could have gone a completely different way.

Clasping her wrists with one strong hand he raised his weapon once more to her head.

"Are you always this feisty?" Her eyes widened as she inhaled sharply.

The expression on his face, along with the chilling way his eyes roamed over her, just like Aiden. But Aiden didn't have a brother, did he?

"You see it now, don't you?" She wished she were able turn over and puke.

"I-I don't understand."

"You don't need to." Unable to worm out of his steely hold she watched as his fingers wrapped around the trigger, closed her eyes, and heard a shot.

People around her screamed… and nothing. She opened her eyes. The mystery man clutched his arm, blood oozing through the long sleeve of his grey shirt.

"I'll be seeing you again, *Cassidy*." How did he know her name?

The men ran as more shots rang out. She turned to see a well dressed Mercer standing there, weapon drawn. Surely there was a good explanation for his presence. Whatever the reason, she had no interest.

"I've been trying to call you for the past two weeks!" She frowned.

"I noticed."

"Why didn't you answer?"

"Our business is finished, there's nothing left to talk about." He shook his head in disbelief as she somehow swayed to her feet.

"Are you drunk?"

"Who cares? I don't work for you, and I bloody well deserve to be!"

Her brother and the women watched the exchange in stunned silence, unsure of what to make of the situation. She stumbled to the wall, leaning against it for support. Why were there now three of him? He released a heavy sigh.

"Look, we need to discuss a few things, including Chase." Her head shot up so fast she nearly threw up in her mouth.

"We don't need to talk about anything, especially Chase! I've been to four funerals. FOUR! And I *don't* want to think about another one!"

"Cassy, what are you talking about?" Joe chimed in, placing a hand on her shoulder.

She ignored him, shrugging away.

"How did you find me?"

"Your phone, and Chase..."

"Just shut it! I..." She couldn't finish the sentence.

Her stomach gave up its contents, some landing on the Sergeant Majors' shoes. Without a word he grabbed some tissue from a pocket of his black dress pants and wiped it away before throwing the refuse in a nearby garbage receptacle.

"I can see this is a bad time. I'll stop by your place tomorrow. Hopefully you'll be in a more reasonable frame of mind."

What? Hell no!

"No! I..." He waved a hand in dismissal.

"Night, Miss Macayla." He hopped in a black vehicle and was gone in a flash.

"What was that about?" Joe pressed.

"I don't want to talk about it."

"You can't..."

"Just drop it, Joe!" She stared in warning.

"Let's just go." Sheila offered.

Cassidy shook her head in disagreement.

"Let me go home, you guys can stay, do whatever you want. I should have just stayed home."

Joe and Sheila peered at each other as if reading each other's minds. Cassidy opened her mouth to inquire about their relationship but stopped when Joe spoke.

"I'll go with you."

"I'll be by later." Sheila added.

He gave an affirmative nod. Spying a taxi nearby they jumped in.

"Talk to you later." Sheila called to him.

He waved back.

"Yep."

The driver pulled away after receiving the address.

"So what's going on between you and Sheila?" He shifted in his seat, uneasy.

"It's… complicated." His tone discouraged further questioning.

Awkward silence followed. Katy Perry's voice bellowed through the speakers about how she'd rise, and Cassidy wondered at the possibility given the depth of her pain. If she had an angel out there, she could definitely use their help.

Despite her best efforts, her mind kept returning to Mercer's arrival, just in the nick of time. Had he become aware someone was after her? How did her assailant know where to find her? Was he truly somehow related to Aiden?

The more she thought, the less things made sense. Aiden remained behind bars in a military prison, his crimes broadcasted on nearly every news station across the country. How could anyone sympathize with him? Surely even his relatives had some common sense. Wasn't his level of treason punishable by death?

"Let's just catch a movie on Netflix when we get back." She turned to Joe.

"Sounds good."

Chapter Two

Chase

"She thinks you're dead."

"WHAT?" That certainly explained her absence.

He sat upright. For the past two weeks he waited in that hospital bed for her to come. Every day, disappointment. He wondered if she cared anymore, if she considered him worth the effort, if she reconsidered, or she'd actually played him. Now he understood. A curse escaped his lips.

"I was under the impression you planned to tell her."

The Sergeant paced the private room, head hung low.

"I've been trying for two weeks, but she refuses to answer my calls. Tracked her to a dance club last night, but she was piss drunk. You should realize, she was right outside your room at the other hospital when it exploded, was unaware you were already gone. Been trying to explain, no luck."

Chase ran a hand over his head, tubes tugging at his skin.

"You still plan to tell her?"

"I planned to today, but something came up, and I want to discuss it with you."

His ears perked up.

"What is it?"

"The laptop, we're in, and there's more people involved than we originally assumed."

"Who?"

"Tony, Aiden's brother."

That got his attention.

"Where is he?"

"We haven't figured that out, but right now, they're all under the impression you're dead."

He stared, shocked.

"You mean our enemies, as well as Cassidy, all assume I'm dead."

"Yeah, and in order to find them, you might need to stay that way for a while."

Heaving a sigh he ran a hand over his head once more. This did nothing to set his mind at ease. Poor Cassidy.

"I'll be out in two days. What am I supposed to do?"

"You have a picture or anything of him?"

"No, they were home."

Aiden was lucky to get locked up before he found out it was him who rigged the explosives in his home. If he'd have gotten his hands on the bastard, his face would be the last thing Aiden ever saw.

"OK." The Sergeant walked to a briefcase next to the visitor chair, opened it, pulled out a folder.

"Here. Study this. I want you to find out how he's getting this information, and where he's sending it."

Chase opened the folder. Page after page, stolen strategies and battalion placements for their next mission, aircraft and weapons schematics, and more. Near the end was a list of possible contact names for Aiden's faction, all unknown save for Tony. His jaw tensed.

"Where did this come from?"

"The laptop."

Cassidy had really done them a service turning that over. It also put her life in danger. Shit...

"Find out if any of them are local. Numbers, addresses, everything you can. If nothing else, start with Tony."

"I have no resources if I'm dead. How?"

"You're one of my best agents with a gift for stealth and subterfuge. If anyone can do it, it's you. I'll have my government contacts help you if necessary."

"Anything else on there?"

"We're still working on it."

"If the rest of them possess the knowledge that Cassidy retrieved the laptop, they'll likely track her down and kill her."

"I know. I may still stop by and tell her to watch her back. Hopefully that'll keep her sober enough to stay vigilant."

"Will you tell her about me?"

"No, and I suggest you don't either. Can't take any chances. I want them found, apprehended, and tried. I want enough dirt on them that they can't walk, and I'm making it your job to dig. If she knows, once they get her, they'll know."

"Yes, Sir."

Mercer handed him a slip of paper with an address.

"This motel room is rented under an alias. Once out, that's where you go. You'll have clothing, a laptop, food, everything you need."

"Understood, Sir."

"Good. I'll check back later." Chase watched him go.

His heart ached for Cassidy. All this time he thought she'd ditched him, and all along she presumed he died. He couldn't imagine her pain.

Sergeant Major was right. While it was only a matter of time before they found her, he had to take care of business. He hoped he got them before they got her.

He retrieved his mp3 player from the nightstand, popping the ear-buds in his ears. Godsmack screamed Awake in his brain. He'd track them down, they'd get what they deserved. Instinct told him Tony would be the first to attempt to get at Cassidy. He'd tear him apart if he tried. They had no idea what was coming and would regret the day they turned traitor.

Chapter Three

Cassidy

Chase ran a hand through her silken honey tresses. Clenching a fistful, he tilted her head back with a sharp tug, extracting a gasp from her lips. With hungry ferocity his mouth consumed hers as his free hand explored her aching body. Fire ignited within, searing every inch of her.

"Oh Chase, I never thought I'd see you again." She barely got the words out.

"I'll never leave you behind, not again. Never again." Hearing that, knowing he meant it, filled her with more joy than she ever imagined possible.

A wall of flames encompassed them in a sudden burst, explosions erupted all around. Fearfully she scanned their surroundings, clutching his shirt. Another look at Chase, now riddled with bullets, gushing blood, and nearly dismembered.

She screamed, unable to stop, even when her voice had gone, she couldn't stop. Tears flooded her face. Once more she was alone, enveloped in darkness, the stench of burning debris and scorched flesh all that remained.

Cassidy awoke drenched in sweat, pressing a hand to her temple against the throbbing pain in her head. It felt like somebody might be crunching a typewriter in there. The bright sun beaming through the window, searing her eyes, only worsened the problem. With a groan she arose and headed to the adjoining bathroom.

The dream was still fresh, leaving her fighting the moisture building behind her eyes. Demons haunting her dreams was nothing new. Chase frequenting her dreams, also familiar, but never had she imaged he'd become one of them. It tore at her soul unlike anything she'd ever known.

With the tub full she sank into the steaming water. Her mind conjured up hazy memories of the night before, followed by a long string of questions. Who was the man that attacked her? Could he be Aidens' brother, or was it just a fluke?

Once the water had cooled she rinsed, dried, and dressed. A loud crash sent her heart racing as she rushed downstairs. Nothing in the guest bedroom, everything was in order in the kitchen, she halted at the living room. Joe wrapped in a blanket, huddled against the arm of the couch, shaking and sweating profusely. On the coffee table was a sandwich bag half-full of pills, a bottle of water, a spoon, syringe needle, and a lighter.

Panic bubbled fiercely.

"I thought you said you're trying to get clean! What's all this?" She stormed toward him.

"I am! I haven't had any in a while, I'm croaking here!"

Uncertainty ran rampant. Withdrawals were no laughing matter, and she didn't want to be too hard on him. She'd become acquainted with drugs before, for her it stemmed from depression and heartache.

"What should I do?"

"Call Sheila. She has the day off."

"What's her number?"

He pulled a small notebook out from beneath his blanket, handed it to her. She marched to the phone on the counter in the kitchen and dialed.

"Hello?"

"Sheila? It's Cassidy. Joe wants you over right away. He's withdrawing pretty bad and needs your help." A sigh escaped the receiver.

"Alright, I'll be there in about twenty minutes."

"Thanks."

Returning to Joe she sat beside him, wrapping an arm affectionately around him.

"I'm sorry, Cassy. I don't mean to be so much trouble."

"Shh. Don't worry. I'll help you. As long as you really want to get clean, I'm here for you, all the way."

"I appreciate that. I know things aren't easy for you."

He couldn't begin to understand.

"Don't worry about it."

Just over twenty minutes later someone knocked on her door. She answered.

"Thanks for coming."

"No problem."

They made their way to the living room. Sheila inhaled sharply.

"Oh God!"

Cassidy watched as Sheila rushed to his side.

"You know we can get you on Methadone. There's no need for you to suffer like this!"

"No! I don't care if it's a weaker substitution, I don't want to trade one addiction for another!"

"Well, we can try naturally if you want, but cold turkey won't help your murmur."

Cassidy cringed at the thought of what effect this might have on his heart.

"I know, I know..."

"What do you want to do?"

"What should I do?" Sheila appeared surprised by his question.

"If you don't want the Methadone or professional help, the natural method might be the only way."

"OK." Had he really agreed?

Addicts rarely behaved so reasonably. What sway did Sheila have over him?

"Tell me what you need, I'll get it for him."

Sheila wasted no time telling her.

"A well balanced diet with plenty of water. Supplementation. He needs a full spectrum of vitamins and minerals, 5-HTP, melatonin, ashwagandha, Saint John's wart, whatever helps him rebuild and replenish his neurotransmitters. Also some Immodium for a less than pleasant symptom."

Sounded like an expensive undertaking, but she'd do whatever necessary to help him in his recovery. After all, she was no stranger to suffering.

"Alright, I can get those. Anything else?"

"He'll need warm baths, plenty of sleep, I'll help with those. Right now you should make him something to eat. He can take one of his pills with his meal and a full glass of water. That should help for a bit."

"I'm on it."

A half hour later she presented him a plate of poached eggs on toast with steamed asparagus, sliced avocado, and wedges of cantaloupe.

Sheila nodded her approval.

"Thank you." Joe muttered before picking at the food on his plate.

He didn't appear to have much of an appetite, but tried as Sheila offered gentle encouragement.

"There you go. Here now, take this." A pill from his bag. "Drink as much water as you can. When you're ready, we can run you a bath." Joe nodded timidly.

"Great." Sheila smiled warmly.

A solid pounding on the front door startled her. With caution she answered. Mercer. It took effort to be polite. She was in no mood to see him, or anything that reminded her of Chase.

"Hope you're feeling better this morning, Miss Macayla."

"Of course, thank you. Come in."

As she opened up for him he entered, followed her to the kitchen, both then took a seat at the table.

"Is there something I can do for you, Sergeant? Can I get you a drink?"

"No, thank you." He shook his head. "We managed to get into the laptop."

The contents of the laptop were no business of hers, but she'd be lying if she said she wasn't curious.

"And?"

"Of course I won't reveal any details as to what's on it, but there's reason to believe your life is in danger." Again?

She sighed. Did this have anything to do with the guy that looked so much like Aiden? Impossible. A fluke, nothing more. Besides, if it were so, surely Mercer would have said something.

"With all due respect, Sir, if you're going to ask me to go into some witness protection program, forget it. Anyone who might be aware of my involvement in your odd little plan has been locked up, and I'm not going to live in fear because somebody somewhere might want to hurt me. Anyway, I can handle myself."

He considered his words. Perhaps he understood there'd be no swaying her.

"Be careful, vigilant. You have no idea what awaits, and one wrong move might mean your life."

Her eyes narrowed. *I'll be seeing you again, Cassidy.* A chill ran down her spine. A sense of darkness loomed. In those few words from Mercer's mouth she realized a great deal remained unsaid, including something big. She sensed he wouldn't add to that. What she wouldn't give to have Chase back. She swallowed against the threatening tears.

"Understood, Sir." He stood. "Anything else?"

"No, nothing else. Have a good day, Miss Macayla."

She followed behind him on the way to the entrance, reached around him, opened the door. He turned to her.

"I'll be in touch." All she could muster was a nod.

What was he hiding? He walked out, and she closed the door behind him.

"What was that about?" Joe stood at the entrance to the living room, looking much more lively.

"I think things are about to get rocky." Heavy music flowed from the room behind him. "What are you listening to?"

"What? Oh, that's 'Get Up' by Korn and Skrillex."

Her eyebrows scrunched in confusion.

"How does that help you? Why not something a little more calming, like classical or something?" She didn't hate the song, but didn't understand playing something adrenaline inducing when relaxation would be most beneficial, given the circumstances.

He chuckled, smiled.

"Motivational music."

"Right..."

"Whatever works." Sheila called out from the black leather couch.

Peering behind him she could see her head banging to the music.

With a chuckle, she joined them, but her mind kept looping around Mercers' warning.

She had her brother, and there certainly seemed to be something between him and Sheila. Cassidy had... something. It might be a shell of what she had before, but it was better than nothing. Even so, her heart desired Chase more than her next breath. If only she'd have died instead. She'd trade his place in a heart beat.

Chapter Four

Chase

"You're a free man now. How does it feel?" Doctor Robert ran a hand through his short raven hair, charcoal eyes revealing his humor, a smile on his youthful looking face.

"Amazing, thanks, doc. You've made me a believer in miracles." Not quite, but being brought back from death was still quite a feat.

He attributed it mostly to Cassidy. He couldn't leave her, not if he had any say. That, and a desire for revenge. The man chuckled.

"Just doing my job." Chase rose from the office chair facing the mahogany desk and shook the doctors' hand.

Even though they were the same age, there was no questioning the man's abilities based on the two rows of degrees and certificates lining the wall behind him.

"Great job. Don't get insulted when I say I hope I don't see you any time soon."

"None taken." Chase made his way to the door, overnight bag in hand.

"Take care, Mister Averey."

"Will do."

The dismissal came late, but with good reason. He worked best under the cover of darkness. He reached the outside of the well concealed military hospital, made it around the corner, then bumped into the Sergeant Major.

"Here." Chase retrieved a set of keys from his hand.

"There's a car in the lot just ahead. Black with tinted windows. You'll find a change of clothes in the trunk, surveillance and recording equipment, and weapons. Go to the motel, everything else is there. Got it?"

"Yes, Sir." Temptation to inquire about Cassidy flooded him, he hesitated.

"Cassidy's fine."

Chase offered a curt tilt of his chin.

"Thank you."

About forty minutes later he reached the motel, a decrepit nothing of a place right off the highway, surrounded by forest for miles. Nearly half the letters on the illuminated sign didn't even work. Not another car in the lot, and the lobby appeared vacant. Perfect.

He grabbed everything from the trunk, wasting no time getting inside the room. It was clean, nary a speck of dust, barely furnished, but still a musty scent lingered. One queen-sized bed, an old wooden nightstand with an ancient looking alarm clock, and a stand against the wall opposite the bed with a television that could have been from the 80's. The mini fridge in the corner near the bathroom was obviously new.

On the bed was a laptop case and two large duffel bags. He searched them. Clothing, toiletries, boxing gear. Perplexed, he gave the room another look, this time checking under the bed. A large Everlast bag. He couldn't help but grin. One of the Sergeant Major's many ways of telling him not to get sloppy.

Memories of sparring sessions with Cassidy surfaced. The look and feel of her glistening skin, the one and only time they shared a bed together. Unlike anything he expected. The sound of her pleasure was like salve to his ears. Eagerness permeated every part of his body with the hope that it wouldn't be the last, wanting to know just what surprises he'd earn if given the chance. Once this was over, she'd hopefully welcome him back, assuming she didn't move on. Hopefully not. Extra incentive to get this over with as quickly as possible.

Opening the laptop case he pulled out the laptop, an external hard drive, several USB sticks, and finally the charger. In seconds he was online. He grabbed the file folder from his overnight bag, then set to work searching the names, starting with Tony.

A phone rang. A quick search and he found it in a separate section of the laptop case. He looked at the call display. Mercer.

"Hello."

"Good, you've arrived."

"Yes, Sir."

"Got something for you."

"Shoot."

"Holyoke Warf. The Conquering Infinity. Tonight. Twenty-three hundred hours." That gave barely over an hour to be there and ready.

"Understood."

Overnight bag full of equipment, he got there with twenty minutes to spare. Clothed in black from head to toe, he blended in with the night. Wasting no time, he bugged the easy to find, moderate sized boat with microphones and cameras, then settled in an empty warehouse within viewing distance. Setting up his laptop, he plugged in a USB and hit record.

It wasn't long before the first sign of life. Three men dressed in jeans and hoodies walked into the well furnished living area on the lower deck which looked like a throw back to the seventies. Five minutes later, four more joined, dressed in dark clothing. One carried a briefcase.

"About time you got here!"

"Yeah, yeah. Here." One of the hooded men stepped forward, lowered his hood as the man that replied stepped forward.

Each person's entourage kept a hand over their holstered weapons.

Tony opened the briefcase, revealing papers, envelopes, and cash.

"With the loss of our laptop it's only a matter of time before they figure out our plan, what we know, assuming they don't already. We need to change strategies and gather new Intel."

Tony barely concealed his rage.

"You think I don't know that? I'm already on it. This will take time, they'll be changing it as soon as they've got everything. Meanwhile, I'm inside homeland security, thanks to my brother."

"Thought they got him." Tony laughed.

"They can't stop the flow of information, as much as they'd like to think so."

This meant someone working in the facility housing Aiden was leaking information since visitors were not permitted to see him. Was Tony a hacker, or employing one?

"Did you take care of the woman?"

Tony's eyes flashed danger.

"My problem, not yours. She'll be easy pickings since Agent Averey got blown to hell." Chase couldn't help but smirk. He wondered if Tony was responsible for what happened at the hospital. "I've seen her. She's a shell of her former self." That sent guilt tearing through his gut.

Why hadn't he gotten her number while he still had the chance?

"Shouldn't we be trying to get info out of her? She must know something. After all, she worked with the Sergeant Major. Isn't that worth putting off revenge?"

Tony roared in frustration.

"She knows nothing and only suspects I'm Aiden's brother. I'd have gotten rid of her too if not for the Sergeant..." Tony thought a moment. "Perhaps you're right. Why else would he track her down to a dance club? He showed up, meddled, they exchanged words, then took off."

"What did you hear?"

Tony snickered.

"Nothing. After getting shot I ran. I was out of earshot, watching from my car."

"Shit. OK."

The roar of an approaching vehicle stole his attention. Had they picked up on it too?

"We need to go. Load up the artifacts in the truck, let's move." They started toward the dock. "Tony, call me when you've got the Ice." So they weren't only smuggling artifacts, but Meth as well.

"Count on it."

Chase snapped pictures as they loaded the massive cargo truck. He didn't stop until they were out of sight, making sure to get the license plate. He packed up, took his time getting to the boat, making sure he didn't get spotted.

While his superior would certainly appreciate this, he'd need more. After retrieving his equipment from the boat he wasted no time getting back to his car. His stomach rumbled. No time for that. Keeping his lights off he drove at a crawl toward the exit.

Hearing the same loud engine as before he stopped. Around a corner up ahead the truck pulled out, followed by a blue SUV. He followed the vehicles some distance behind. The truck turned one way, the SUV the other. Certain that Tony drove the SUV, he pursued, maintaining a cautious distance behind, lights still off.

Twenty minutes ticked by before Tony slowed down, in South Portland. A familiar area. His blood ran cold when he saw why. Tony pulled into a nearly deserted gas station lot as Cassidy walked around the corner of the store, heading toward the back. What to do. Getting involved would risk his entire mission. If he listened to Mercer, she was as good as dead. Tony got out, other men behind him. They quickly trailed behind her.

With a roar of frustration he drove around back, parking by a fence beneath some low hanging branches, away from the lights of the store. He needed a plan, quick. Running along the wall, he bumped into someone coming out of the back door hauling two large garbage bags. He discreetly grabbed a bottle hanging from a bag.

"Sorry, man."

"No problem."

In seconds the worker returned inside, a song flowing from within, Don't Let Me Down. He stuck the bottle at the bottom edge of the door to keep it open. A scream rang out. Cassidy!

He quickly tied the black bandanna from his pocket around his mouth and nose and pulled his hood up as far as possible without obstructing his sight. With haste he proceeded near to Cassidy while still residing in the concealment of shadow, pulling a slingshot from his back pocket.

"Leave me alone or I'll rearrange the features on each of your faces!" Cassidy, his strong, courageous, foolish woman.

The men laughed.

"I was going to kill you, but it seems someone wants information from you. So we'll let you live... just long enough to give it."

"Bite me!"

"Don't tempt me." One of the men flanking Tony spoke.

"Oh Chase, it looks like I'll be joining you shortly." It may have been the faintest whisper, but he heard.

Peering around the corner he could see her against the wall, gun drawn, aiming at Tony. Her bags of purchases rested on the ground on either side of her. She remained on the losing end since they also trained their firearms on her. He had to be smart. Avoiding detection by Tony and his entourage remained the only allowable outcome. He picked up a decent sized rock and set it in the pocket of his soundless weapon.

Aiming his slingshot at Tony's SUV parked a few feet behind them, he fired. The front passenger window shattered. Using the distraction he swiftly grabbed Cassidy, covered her mouth to prevent her from screaming, and pulled her around the corner before they had a chance to see him. By the time they rounded the corner, he was inside, door shut, locked.

She spun around quickly, gun trained on him. Tony spoke true, she did look like a shell of her former self. Her eyes were so dull, so lifeless, it shredded his heart. He stepped forward, she backed away.

"Move again, and your gray-matter will decorate the walls."

Chapter Five

Cassidy

Who was this guy? Tall, muscular, stealthy as a panther, darkly dressed head to toe. Did he come to help her, or them? If the latter, he'd soon learn he tangled with the wrong woman.

She took in the storage room, large, packed, and dull grey. Moving backwards in the dim light, she searched for the door. A fraction of a second. That's all it took from the time she turned her head to the moment he pinned her against the wall.

Moving her arms overhead, he held her wrists firmly with one strong hand, taking her gun with the other, propping his knee between hers, anticipating her next move, groin shot. He pressed his hips against hers, pinning her completely against the wall. One of Chase's moves during sparring matches. She swallowed against the sadness wrapping around her heart.

She spun out of his grasp, ducking around him. Like lightning she wrapped an arm around his throat, pulling down, securing her hold. Once air tight, she fell back to the ground, wrapped her legs around his waist, closing her ankles together.

To her astonishment, he stood up. Her hold tightened. He separated her ankles and in the blink of an eye her back was to the ground, wrists secured above her head, his knee once again between her legs. Looking up she caught a mischievous pair of crisp, ocean-blue eyes focusing on her, the evidence of his arousal pressing hard into her thigh. Suddenly, she forgot how to breathe. Her eyes widened. No way, it couldn't be. Did she dare hope?

In her moment of weakness he ripped down the bandanna, revealing his face, complete with a five o'clock shadow. Most men weren't able to pull that off, but he did, in spades. Her heart soared. How was it possible? Words failed her.

His mouth crushed hers, consuming, as though starved for oxygen and she monopolized the entire supply. Her body liquefied beneath him. His hold on her loosened and she wrapped her arms tight around his neck, pulling him in deeper, as if that would keep him safe, keep him from disappearing again.

When Edwin McCain started on the store radio, he released her. I'll Be, a song she hadn't listened to in forever. Chase scanned her features before settling on her eyes.

"I think I just found our song." She struggled for words.

"You're alive! I - I thought you were..."

"Yeah, I heard, I was..." She gaped. "For about twenty minutes."

She had no idea to whom, but she owed someone a debt of gratitude she could never afford to repay. Tears welled in her eyes as her heart soared ever higher. She sat up and ran a hand over his cheek.

"I'm so sorry! If I'd have known you were alive, I'd have looked for you! I'd..." Voices grew closer.

She recognized them. Chase grabbed her arm, lifted her up.

"I know. We need to get out of here." He pulled up his bandanna and flipped his hood far over his head, then returned her weapon.

"Sorry Sir, that room is employees only." Cassidy held her breath.

"I don't care. Let me in before I add an extra hole in your head!"

Chase opened the back door, they were out, door closed, just as the men barged in. They bolted to Chases' car. She froze.

"What about my stuff?" Chase appeared confused. "The stuff I just bought for my brother."

Funny how she cared more about that than her own vehicle. Of course, the men who were after her probably already had it. Good thing she carried nothing valuable in there. He shook his head.

"He'll have to wait. You'll have to get it somewhere else. Get in." She immediately did as instructed.

It was obvious he didn't want to abandon what he was doing, but understood that if they saw him with her, it would end in disaster. He'd taken every precaution to avoid detection. After some distance, ensuring no one followed, he lowered his hood and bandanna, then asked.

"You started talking to your brother?" She nodded.

"He came knocking. Probably a good thing too, he saved my life."

A strange looked crossed his face.

"How?"

She gulped.

"Umm, not important." His expression intensified, but he said nothing.

"I find it interesting the first time I see you is right in the nick of time. It's almost like you were following them." He looked shocked, but quickly schooled his features.

"Yeah, I was." He seemed unsure about something.

She should have known he'd be right back to work, if she'd realized he was alive. At least it wasn't overseas. It would kill her if he had to go away. A frown formed on her face. If only he'd retire.

"Can you tell me what's going on?"

"They think I'm dead, that you have information from Mercer useful for their cause, and after they get that, they're going to kill you." She frowned.

Would she ever be safe again? Bad enough having to worry about Steve, her homicidal ex. She had no idea how she'd be able to face him in court.

"You must know something about them, at least one in particular."

"What do you mean?"

"The guy that looks a lot like Aiden. This is the second time he came after me."

His eyes widened.

"When was the first?"

"A couple of days ago. Only, that time he was hell bent on shooting first and forgoing any questions."

"I see. That would be Tony, Aiden's brother." So her assumptions were correct.

"I never met him before this."

Chase's jaw tightened, lips forming a thin line.

"I have, a number of times." He growled. "I never realized Aiden was such a spineless maggot. We've been friends for years. All this time, he was playing fucking Judas!" He punched the door so hard she nearly jumped out of her skin. "Why would he do that? Son of a bitch qualifies for extinction!"

Anger poured from his face, matching the venom drenching his words, warning her into silence. Knowing Aiden wasn't trustworthy from the get-go didn't make her feel any better. It hurt to know Chase endured so many stabs to the back, but there was nothing she could do. She sat in sombre silence. A few seconds passed.

"Can you guess who destroyed my house?" Her eyes widened as her head spun toward him with a gasp.

"Umm... A-Aiden?" It barely came out a whisper.

"Lucky he's rotting in prison right now because if I'd have gotten my hands on him, he wouldn't live to tell." She swallowed, fell back in silence, shifting her focus to the forest scenery outside her window.

The rage emanating from him seemed almost tangible, she could feel it as though her own, like a consuming fire. Never did she want to be on the receiving end of his ire. Silenced loomed for a while, and his eyes burned through her.

"I'm sorry if I scared you. I didn't mean to."

When she turned she saw guilt etched in his face. She sighed.

"You didn't. I just... I don't know how to explain it. When you're angry, I guess I kinda sense it more than most. It's intense, and I never want to be the reason for it, never want you to feel that way." He ran a gentle finger down her cheek.

"Bad things happen, can't always stop it, but having you makes me happy. I wouldn't trade you for anything. You're safe with me, I promise." She wanted to believe him, but her foot in mouth disease was sporadic, and sometimes downright devastating.

"It's OK, sweetheart, you're here with me now. I got you."

How was he able to say the sweetest, most incredible things in that rich honeyed tone at the most interesting moments? No wonder women fawned over him! If he weren't driving she'd have kissed him. She nipped her lip. OK, perhaps she'd have done more than that. How'd she get so lucky? He left her breathless, speechless.

Fidgeting in her seat, she reached for the volume control. His hand covered hers, stopping her.

"We can just drive quietly, no need to talk. It's not awkward for me."

The smoothness of his voice caressed her ears and the warmth of his skin as his thumb sparked a trail across the flesh of her hand fogged her mind. How did he read her so easily? It didn't seem fair. He crooked a smile that created knots in her stomach and made her pulse quicken.

"Where are we going?"

"I can drive you to a different store, then take you home if you'd like." As much as she wanted to stay with him, she couldn't let her brother down.

She exhaled in dismay.

"Yeah, that's probably a good idea." He released her hand, leaving the skin prickling in protest.

He smiled warmly.

"That's what we'll do then."

Nearly a half hour later she made it home with at least some of what Joe needed. Reaching the front door, her back snapped straight, whole body charged on adrenaline. Light penetrated through the sliver of the barely open door. She set down her parcels and retrieved her gun, all while Chase remained parked in the driveway just before the garage door.

Seeing her cautious approach, he jumped into action. He was at her side, hood and bandanna on once more. Relief filled her that he didn't ask questions, fearing someone might still be there. Last thing they needed was for someone to hear them.

It was strange to see Chase go into commando mode as he entered first, gun in hand, but she trusted him and didn't want to disappoint. She followed with a gasp. To say there were signs of a struggle would be an understatement. The place was a disaster. Broken furniture strewn about, holes in the walls, blood spatter everywhere, she wasn't sure if she wanted to scream or cry. Maybe both. Joe was a bit of a brawler, so she understood not all the blood was his.

He started making signals, at first leaving her confused. She shook her head, holding back a chuckle. Did he forget she wasn't military? Still she tried. He held up a hand so she waited. When he pointed toward the kitchen she went cautiously. Where were Joe and Sheila? Nothing in the kitchen. She headed upstairs.

Three bedrooms and no sign of life. Time for the attic. Nothing there either, not even in the alcove behind the bookshelf. She had the thing mechanically fused to the wall after what happened, only movable by the push of a button beneath the floor board, an idea she credited to Mercer and his safe-house.

Near the bottom of the stairs, Chase met her, page in hand. Her blood froze as she read.

Since you like to play hardball, we will too. Either you come with us, or your brother and friend are dead. If we don't hear from you by Friday, we start cutting digits.

Joe wouldn't go without a fight, and if they did get him, it didn't go easily for them.

A phone number was scrawled at the bottom of the page. Rage coursed through her veins like wildfire as her body vibrated uncontrollably. She never got the term 'seeing red' because when angry, like now, she only ever saw black. She crumbled the page but Chase grabbed it before it got destroyed.

"That's a hand written note, which makes it evidence."

"What am I going to do?"

"You're coming with me to the motel. Then, I'll report to Mercer."

"I don't get it! I don't have any information, or anything they might possibly want."

"Yeah, you do." Her brows furrowed, confused.

"What are you talking about?"

"Other than the fact you managed to get that laptop to Mercer, they are aware you still communicate with the Sergeant Major. Then there's whatever you got during my last seizure, that I'm casual for a branch of homeland security, and me. They think I'm dead. You know I'm not." Her lips parted, surprised. "If they find out I'm alive, that changes everything. It's imperative they don't." Mercer must have informed him he'd told her more about his other employ.

Her shoulders slumped in despair. Poor Joe! Depending on how bad his murmur was, his withdrawals could kill him. If nothing else, it would likely damage his heart further.

"We have to do something! I've lost so much, I don't want to lose my brother too! I only just got him back!"

"He'll at least be fine until Friday." She growled in frustration.

"You don't get it! He's trying to get off a drug addiction to Oxycontin, and he has a heart murmur. If his withdrawal symptoms don't get managed properly, he could... he could..." He seemed to understand and wrapped his arms around her.

"Shh..." He petted her head. "We'll do what we can, but right now, we have to go. We'll talk to Mercer, see what he says. It's the only thing we can do at the moment."

She knew if things weren't done Chase's way she'd put more than just her brother's life at stake, but didn't see any other way to save Joe than give them what they wanted. Being in jail wouldn't help either, which is probably what would happen if she tried to deal with them herself. If the opportunity ever presented itself, she'd kill Tony with her bare hands.

She bit her tongue on telling him he should have let her die. The idea of finishing what she'd started the night Joe showed up was tempting. Begrudgingly, she gathered her purchases and stormed to his vehicle.

"Let's go." She ground out.

Once inside, she crossed her arms, pouting. She didn't care how childish she appeared, she was in a no-win situation. Sirens echoed in the distance, growing louder. She realized the situation. They had to make themselves scarce before the police arrived. At least her neighbors were on the ball this time. Rage continued to roar through her veins.

She cranked up the volume of the radio. Katy's voice ripped through the speakers. Rise, the same song as a couple of nights ago when Aiden's brother first attacked her. If she ever got her hands on the men responsible, they'd learn the full meaning behind 'hell hath no fury like a woman scorned'.

Chapter Six

Chase

Unthinkable. After everything she endured, now this. It was enough to drive anybody insane. She merely sat there, arms crossed, staring intently at the overcast clouds the entire drive. Never before had he seen her so angry. Other people would have given up on life by now, and if he understood correctly, a few nights ago, she almost did. Hopefully she wouldn't do anything reckless.

Cassidy wasted no time getting out of the vehicle upon arrival, but waited for him to lead the way to his room. Not a moment too soon, with a clasp of thunder it started pouring the moment they reached the door. After entering, she set her bags beneath the window beside the entrance, then dropped on the bed.

She spied the Everlast bag propped against the wall.

"You have any other equipment with you?"

How could he forget what happened during their stay at the safe-house? She'd laid into that bag as though it contained the source of all her pain. He'd have to be heartless not to feel bad for her.

"Yeah, but I haven't found the mount for it yet."

She scanned the room as he removed his hooded shirt and peered over when it landed beside her. A blush crept in her cheeks and the corner of her lips twitched when she realized he caught her staring. Angry as she was, she could easily feed a man's ego with just a look.

"I don't suppose you'll let me help you forget your problems again, for a little while?" She snickered.

"You hiding another death from me?" Oh shit...

"I'm sorry, I was only trying to protect you. I didn't know how you'd handle the news. You were already hanging by a thread, I didn't want to send you over the edge. How did you find out?"

With a slow shake of her head she sighed.

"Aiden. A word of advice. Never leave it for your nemesis to tell your girlfriend bad news. I'm sure you were probably trying to protect me somehow, or concerned about my mental state. Still, I'd rather hear it from you."

An unexpected warning. He gulped.

"Won't happen again."

"Thank you." Wow, she really was letting him off easy, but he knew better than to push for it any further.

He tucked his bags under the bed, then sat beside her, retrieving the cell from his pocket.

"I'll give the Sergeant Major a call. It's possible he might want a word with you."

"Good idea."

Nerves rattled, he dialed the number. He wasn't fool enough to think he'd get off so easy with Mercer. Risking life and mission for a woman wasn't something that usually went over well in his line of work. Not that he'd been in this position before, but any form of reckless conduct could mean his job, at best. Mercer answered on the fifth ring.

"Agent Averey, what's the skinny?"

He swallowed. Here goes...

"I have audio and visual documentation, Sir. Ready to deliver."

"Excellent. Anything else to report?" Muscles in his jaw worked as his mind raced.

How was the best way of telling your superior that you defied his order and risked a mission for a female? He groaned inwardly.

"We have a situation."

"What is it?"

"I have Cassidy, err, Miss Macayla, in protective custody, Sir." The anger in the man's voice was unmistakable.

"What the hell happened? Such disregard is uncharacteristic of you, agent. You best get explaining!"

Chase swallowed, gritted his teeth, ignoring the searing feeling of

Cassidy's eyes on his face.

"I was in pursuit of the target when he targeted Cassidy. Their intent was to capture, interrogate, and kill. Intervention was successful. There's another issue to deal with." Mercer's frustrated sigh reached his ears.

"You're just on a roll tonight, Averey. Of all people, I never thought you'd fuck up worse than a Rainbow. Out with it!"

He was sure new recruits had done worse, but knew better than to argue.

"They're holding her brother and someone else hostage and refuse to release them unless she exchanges herself."

"For Christ's sake! You sure you weren't discovered?" Chase continued hurriedly, hoping the explanation would decrease the man's ire.

"Stayed frosty, Sir. The note left for Cassidy was addressed to her only. They have no idea I'm still alive." A growl tore through the phone.

"I'm on my way. For the love of God, don't do anything else reckless!"

Cassidy's gasp told him she'd heard. She paled. The sharp click in his ear told him the call was over. It went better than expected. He still had a job. The unexpected leniency surprised him.

"I got you in trouble?"

"Don't worry about it."

"But..."

"Don't. Worry." He could see the wheels turning in her head.

"Excuse me." She mumbled, displeasure apparent, as she made way to the bathroom.

Forty minutes later Mercer's stern expression greeted him at the door.

"Hope you realize the risk you're taking. If things get FUBAR, it's your ass on a pike!"

Chase straightened.

"I take full responsibility, Sir."

Mercer heaved a sigh at the sight of Cassidy's pale face and startled expression.

"Let me see her note."

Chase retrieved it from his pocket, handed it over. The Sergeant Major shook his head.

"You just invite trouble wherever you go."

He caught the tilt of Mercer's mouth, but Cassidy's anxiety kept her from seeing his humor.

"I'm sorry, I never meant to get Chase in trouble. I honestly thought he was dead!"

Chase let out an exasperated sigh. Mercer ignored her comment and turned to Chase.

"Give me your data." Chase handed him the USB, which Mercer pocketed, along with the note. "If you're sure they haven't seen you, then we can turn your fuck up into an opportunity, that is, if Miss Macayla wants to cooperate."

Cassidy gulped.

"With what...?"

"You call the number, tell them you want to meet. Chase will monitor and record. I'll have men on standby to provide a distraction for your escape if it becomes necessary."

Chase ran his hands anxiously over his head. After what happened last time she played a lure in their plans she got hurt, bad. At least the cuts and bruises that marred her skin had gone, except for the stitches. The last thing he wanted was her getting involved in another dangerous endeavor, but under the circumstances, it was unavoidable.

"I don't think I have a choice."

"Very well." The Sergeant Major pulled a HOP1800 cell with an audio recorder attached and handed it to her.

"This is a disposable cell. We're going for a little drive. You'll call them, then we trash it. Don't worry about how long you're on it, I want to record as much as possible. Understood?" She nodded, eyes on the phone. "Good."

"There's one more thing, Sir." The displeased expression prickled his anxiety, but received a nod to continue. "Cassidy claims she got attacked a couple of nights ago, at a club."

That perked Mercer's interest.

"What of it?"

"I believe it was Tony."

A split second of hesitation preceded a long string of curses.

"Come, Miss Macayla. Let's get this done. I want that son-of-bitch's head on a pike."

Friday night, Chase observed through the clear, starlit night from the same warehouse window as last time, surveillance equipment on the go, looking at Cassidy's fidgety form as she waited for Tony's arrival. Only, instead of the boat, he paid attention to the rundown building across the small expanse of water. He adjusted the controls, plugged in the USB, and squatted.

"Ready." The voice of another agent crackled through his ear piece.

"Stand by." He ordered.

Minutes ticked by, ten, fifteen, twenty... Where were they? Along with his racing heart, instinct told him this wasn't going to end well. A car approaching from his left caught his attention. Finally. Tony, followed by five men, exited, approaching her. Where were the hostages? Tony was first to speak.

"So glad you made it."

Cassidy stared icily.

"Where's my brother? Where's Sheila?" She glanced toward the dark colored car.

"They're around, somewhere. I planned to bring them, but in the midst of my constant pursuit of knowledge, I've discovered something."

Through his binoculars Chase could see the sweat beading down her face despite the coolness of the night, her skin paler than the moonlight.

"I'm in no mood for your games. Give me back my brother!"

Tony stepped closer, nearly an inch from her face, before circling around her, like a predator getting ready to pounce, then ran a finger down her cheek and long sleeve of her soft pink shirt, dangerously close to a breast. Definitely deliberate. His blood singed his veins, muscles burning at the effort to keep from going over there and breaking Tony's neck. Tony stopped before her, taunting eyes burning into her.

"Not yet. See, I've stumbled across some medical files before my arrival. The reason why I'm a bit late. It seems Agent Averey isn't dead after all, but in another hospital. You wouldn't happen to know anything about that, would you? Because it's a game changer."

Cassidy's eyes widened, mouth gaping, her shock matching his own. How did he find out? Who hacked his medical records? At least they weren't updated. He suspected Mercer had something to do with that. It didn't please him that his instincts were correct. This was turning into a real soup sandwich.

"Ch-Chase is alive? Where is he?" Quick thinking and clever, he loved it.

Tony examined her briefly.

"You had no idea?" She shook her head and swallowed.

A pause.

"This is interesting. I'm sure once he's out he'll want to find you. At least, from what my brother tells me." He pinched a lock of her hair between his fingers.

She straightened, clenching her fists at her sides.

"Get to the point." She hissed.

His sinister eyes met hers, leering.

"I think I'll just keep you instead, and when Agent Averey gets out, I can kill two birds with one stone. Literally. In the meantime, I'll get the information you're hiding, and kill boredom at my leisure." Cassidy gasped, a look of horrid disgust pouring from her face.

Tony snapped his fingers and two men built like brick houses approached him.

"Take this little gem to the car. We're heading back."

"Code red. Execute Plan B!" Chase hissed in the mic of his ear piece.

Cassidy withdrew her gun, backing away quickly. The men produced their own firearms, aiming at her. Tony took a step forward, and she turned her aim on him.

"Be smart. Don't you at least want to live long enough to see your boyfriend?"

"Fuck you." She seethed. "I might die, but if I kill you, I'll be doing the whole world a favor!"

"What about your brother?" Her finger tightened around the trigger.

It impressed him how she wasn't easily intimidated, but remembering why left a sour taste in his mouth. The roar of a large vehicle vibrated through the air. A fraction of a second later a runaway transport came into view, barreling right for Tony and his men.

"Fuck! Forget her for now. Let's go!" He glared at her. "Bring him to us or your brother is dead."

They sped away, burning rubber, narrowly escaping the truck. Cassidy jumped through the doorway into the other warehouse, barely avoiding its path as it careened into the water.

"Shit!" He breathed, ripping through the building to the exit. "Cassidy!"

Chapter Seven

Cassidy

Every muscle and bone ached as if the truck hadn't missed. Groaning, she stood, brushing off the dust from her shirt and jeans. Nothing prepared her for that. Her heart lunged through her throat as she fought against surging panic.

They found out Chase survived and refused to release her brother unless she turned him over. What hospital had he stayed in that left Tony afraid to go himself? Must have maintained some pretty high level security. Didn't matter. Her brother and Sheila were still prisoner, and Joe undoubtedly lacked the help he needed. What was she to do?

"Cassidy!" Chase's concerned voiced echoed in the night air.

She rushed out, enveloped by a welcoming pair of steely arms.

"Oh God Chase, what are we going to do?" Her eyes met his, pleading.

"We'll get back to the motel, hand in what we have. Mercer will help us decide after that."

The drive back to the motel was silent at first, save for Skillet screaming about feeling invincible through the speakers. If not for Chase, she didn't know how she would have survived. Just knowing he was there somewhere, watching, ready to step in, made her braver than usual, but she knew Chase would protect her. On top of that, she wanted to kill the man for what he and his men had done to her.

"Thank you."

He glanced over, curious.

"For what?"

"Looking out for me." He ran a hand gently down her cheek.

"We'll do everything possible to save your brother. I won't let anything happen to you either, not if I can help it." Her head tilted into his hand, relishing his touch.

As soon as she got in the door, she collapsed on the bed, watching as Chase made his report. Spying the remote behind the alarm clock, she turned on the archaic television, and froze. Just when she thought things wouldn't get any worse, the smug looking man with salt-and-pepper comb-over hair and beady brown eyes on the screen had to open his mouth.

"Around six this morning, Stephen Melanson escaped South Portland Prison. It's unclear at this time who his affiliations are. An investigation is in progress. Meanwhile, the FBI has issued a warning that he is now considered armed and dangerous. If you do see him, call 911. Do not approach."

Impossible...

"Chase, you don't suppose Aiden's brother had anything to do with that?"

He pocketed his phone.

"Tony? I can't see why, they aren't connected. Unless this has something to do with you."

Something inside told her Tony's hands were all over this. It was beyond her comprehension why he'd do it, and what he gained by busting Steve out. The biggest question hanging in the air was, how had Tony found out about him? She still thought about it when Mercer arrived a half hour later.

"Here's what we have so far." Chase handed over the evidence. "Pretty sure we're dealing with the same hacker that infiltrated your computer."

"Agreed."

Cassidy watched their exchange. She still wondered what on that computer, if anything, led to the attack on the safe-house going the way it went. It would have made more sense if they'd gone through the doors and windows. Why blow a hole in the wall? Especially in the room closest to the one with the weapons cache.

"Miss Macayla, something on your mind?" Mercer's question startled her to present.

"I don't mean to be nosy, I might be crazy, but what was on that computer? I mean, the attackers could have gone through the doors with more weapons than they brought. They seemed so ill prepared."

Mercer grinned, a sparkle in his eyes as he turned to Chase, tilting his head at her.

"Better be careful with this one, she just might be as clever as my Melody."

Confusion mounted. Who's that? She wondered if Chase was a mind reader when he looked at her.

"Melody is - was - his eldest daughter."

Was? Sympathy welled up within. She didn't know what to say.

"I'm sorry." Her mouth wasn't able to formulate anything else.

Curiosity about the woman gnawed at her, but it didn't seem appropriate to ask.

"Don't apologize. My daughter was a wonderful lady. She'd be the first to call me on my shenanigans, the first to pick up on something like that. Just as much intestinal fortitude too."

He still hadn't answered her, and she figured it better not to push.

"Thank you, Sir... I think." Mercer crooked an impish grin, the crack in his usual serious demeanor surprised her.

"I may have had the wrong blue-prints or mislabeled something. Durability, weaknesses, who knows? Who would I be to dangle a carrot in front of a rabbits' nose?"

Something told her Mercer was a crafty man. She smiled.

"OK. Let's dial it back a bit. We have a bigger problem." Chase cut in.

"What is it?"

"Somebody working for Tony, or possibly the man himself, hacked into my medical records. They know I survived, but think I'm still in the hospital. They refuse to turn over the hostages unless Cassidy turns me over. Also, we need to see if there's any connection between them and a recent prison escapee."

"Stephen Melanson? Yes, I have reason to suspect there is. After Aiden made the news, apparently Mister Melanson managed to reach out to his faction, made a deal if they would get him out."

Cassidy gaped, dumbfounded. Why would they bother with Steve?

"For all we know, they might be using him as a distraction, to try to keep the heat off them. Or to find Cassidy and keep an eye on her. If they're supplying him with weapons, they might have also given him a place to lie low."

She swallowed. None of this made sense.

"Why would he try keeping an eye on me when everyone will be looking for him? They'll recognize him as soon as he shows his face."

Those hazel eyes told her there was more to it than reported on the news.

"If involved with them, they'd have covered all their bases. We're talking altering his appearance. Hair dye, contacts, clothing, facial hair. You name it. It's possible to alter your appearance to such a degree only facial recognition software will detect you." Her insides groaned with dread. "The FBI don't get involved for nothing. I just hope they don't interfere."

Mercer's words surprised her.

"What do you mean? Aren't you guys on the same side?"

The men exchanged glances.

"They like to meddle. If this were something simple, we wouldn't be concerned, but if a terrorist group is involved in his escape, then it's an issue we need to deal with."

She fell backwards on the bed.

"This is so confusing. It makes no sense."

"Let me simplify it, then. They want to tighten a net around you. They believe he knows enough about you to anticipate your actions and behavior."

She shook her head, ran her hands over her face in frustration.

"It doesn't matter what the deal is, he's irrational, obsessed, and will come after me himself. He only cares about getting back at me, especially because he knows I'll testify against him. Assuming he finds me he'll try to kill me. Tony won't get anything. I can't tell you how many times he's walked right through my restraining order."

"You don't have the best luck with men, do you?" Chase asked.

She nipped her lower lip to suppress a grin.

"Depends on your outlook, I guess. I'm with you, aren't I."

Chase found it impossible to hold back laughter.

"And look at all the trouble that followed." Her grin widened.

"Worth every minute." He shook his head.

"You must be a masochist."

"Wouldn't you like to know?"

His jaw fell slack, Mercer's eyes widened. She wondered if she took it a little too far. The darkening of his eyes as they cascaded over her body told her no.

"I'll run this in and get back to you. Keep up on those names in the meantime." Mercer made a hasty retreat.

When the door closed, and they were alone, Chase focused on her.

"Would now be one of those times you let loose one of your surprises?"

She played coy.

"Not sure your mind is capable of handling it. Might drive you over the edge..." She could see his mind working, trying to figure out if she was still angry about him withholding information about her old boss, or if she was toying with him.

It amused her to watch him fidget nervously, like he seemed to enjoy doing to do to her. She worked to suppress a smile. She wasn't angry, water under the bridge, but given the nature of his job, figured some forms of play wouldn't fly. Her idea of fun never included pain, only pleasure, but it's happened that her desire to please had taken her far enough beyond her comfort zone to require a new zip code.

If he would enjoy the same, she hoped he wouldn't ask too much. Pain equated to abuse in her mind, so he'd really have to want it for her to concede. She never liked to disappoint.

"Cassidy, are you screwing with me?"

Her lips curled in mischief as she sat up.

"Maybe..."

"You never used to be so..."

"Naughty?"

He approached, movements almost predatory. He quirked his lips in a dangerous grin.

"That sounds about right."

"Nobody gets the 'bad girl' unless they take me seriously." He seemed highly intrigued as he sat beside her.

"What are we talking about here?" He ran a finger along her jaw line, halting beneath her chin.

No doubt she had his full attention.

"We're talking about lifetime commitment and fidelity. As I told you before, I don't do one night stands, and I don't do flings. It's all or nothing. If you can give me that, then it's just about anything you want."

He gasped.

"What, no ménage à trois?" He teased.

She lowered her head, frowned.

"I don't know. That... complicates things." Chase appeared to reflect on her words, and his eyes widened.

She squirmed. That was something she never wanted to repeat. Apparently some men liked to have their fun, but if a woman turned down an equal opportunity, it meant guys could grope and harass her, and when her repeated rejections were unheeded, even if he were physically present, she was on her own. It had left her in some very precarious situations.

It really affects your sense of value when someone's groping you in your boyfriends' presence, and rather than speak up after your repeated rejections, he just sits there beside you, drinking beer, joking and laughing. Was she the only woman crazy enough to turn down a free pass?

"You mean... you used to...?" With a shake of her head she grinned as his jaw hit the floor.

Her cheeks reddened.

"What made you stop?"

"Let's just say I learned a few valuable lessons and leave it at that."

The look in his eyes reminded her of a child with a new favorite toy.

"You don't get jealous?"

Oh boy...

"Of course I do. It's normal, to an extent. But you're a grown man, with a mind of your own, and should care enough not to hurt me. That being said, I want to make you happy and give you every reason not to feel tempted to do so." She inhaled deeply.

She could see his mind at work.

"Holy crap!"

"Yeah, also, trust is very important. I'm hoping that since it seems I can trust you with my life, I can also trust you with everything else. Also, I'd dance on a pole for you, or your lap, wherever, whatever turns your crank. Every once in a while I can do my hair and makeup however you like."

"Wow, I'm so confused. You always seemed so shy when it came to that. I mean, you never flirted back."

"Because I wasn't be sure you wanted a commitment, I had enough reason to assume you only desired a one night stand or something short term. By the time I realized just how serious you were..." She swallowed. "I thought you were dead. I love you, Chase, and want to give you everything."

His hands rubbed across his head, repeatedly, as if his mind couldn't wrap around it.

"What if you're mad at me? Would you withhold sex from me?"

It was impossible to suppress a chuckle.

"If I'm angry, I'm not likely to want it, I'm not sure how anyone could, but I wouldn't do it as a punishment. That's foolish, and in the end, I'd be punishing myself. Why would I want to do that?"

"Wow!" How'd they get to this conversation from a humorous little quip? "When you say anything I want...?"

"Role play, bondage, things like that, but I don't do the pain thing. Just playful fun."

"Why not?"

A frown formed on her lips.

"I would think that obvious after everything I told you."

He lay back on the bed, pulling her on top of him. She squealed in surprise. His arousal pressed hard against the vee of her hips.

"What if I like a little pain? What if I want spanked and whipped, teeth and nails?" This conversation was quickly rousing her anxiety.

"I'm surprised you'd want any of that, given your profession."

"You said anything."

She found his determination nerve-wracking. A sigh of defeat escaped her.

"I'd chain you to the wall and play dominatrix all night long if that's what you wanted." His brows creased, curious.

"What's the problem?"

"I don't want to hurt you." He cracked up, chest rumbling.

"You're adorable!" She stewed in silence.

He rolled over, pinning her to the bed.

"You'd do all of that, for me?"

She offered a slight nod.

"It might be foolish, but I'd make an exception for you, yes. Just... don't leave me hanging if a guy steps out of line and won't take 'no' for an answer."

"Why - why me?"

Color burned her cheeks.

"You underestimate your value." His eyes shone like polished gems.

"How about we play a little game right now?" She took in his conniving expression.

Her pulse quickened.

"What do you have in mind?"

As he reached for his bag, her eyes roamed his body. When he turned back, he had some rope in his hand. She couldn't help wonder what a person in his line of work had to carry.

"What do you say to me tying you down and having my way with you?"

With a gasp her insides erupted in flames. Did he even need to ask?

"Yes, Sir." She purred.

He carefully tied her hands over her head, around one of the posts of the headboard. With ease he slid up her shirt, covering her eyes.

"Hey! I still want to see you!" She squirmed.

His tone came deep, rich, and molten.

"If I've read you correctly, I'm pretty sure you'll like this."

The car ride to the safe-house, when he covered her eyes with his shirt. Embarrassment flushed her skin crimson. He was far more perceptive than should be permissible.

With care he unclipped her bra and slid it over her head. Velvety warmth engulfed one hardened peak, she arched hungrily with a quiet moan as delicious sensations flooded her. Her body protested its release before relishing in delight as he captured the other.

He lavished her body in exquisite torment, his hands, mouth, leaving blazing fire over her skin, and tension coiling below. She pulled against the rope, wanting to touch him, to see him. When he reached the waist of her jeans he opened them, pulled them down.

Once free, he pried her legs apart. Less than a second and his tongue worked at her nub, threatening to send her over the edge. Her hips took on a mind of their own and she could have sworn he laughed.

"Greedy one, aren't you?" He spoke against her heated flesh, then slipped a finger into her weeping core, leaving her panting.

With a moan she pulled harder against the rope, ignoring the burning pain as it bit into her wrists.

"Fuck you're hot when you struggle."

"I - I want to see you, touch you. Please!"

"Soon enough." He teased.

The relentless efforts of his fingers and tongue soon sent her over the edge, a rippling cascade of ecstasy. Her body hummed in contentment and he released her. When her eyes finally adjusted to the light, she watched as he pried a condom from his pocket before tearing off his pants and boxers. Seconds later he had it on and eased in her.

Her breath caught as his steady rhythm roused the fire inside once more. His mouth suffocated hers, his hunger unrestrained as his hands felt every inch of her aching body. Her palms explored his taught frame, fingers playing over hardened ridges of muscle, nails digging in a plea for more as she moaned against his mouth.

His primal groans caressed her ears and vibrated through her spine. The combination of his voice, his touch, left her writhing, the pressure between her hips coiling once more to explosive heights of pleasure. Sparkles burst before her as he thrust harder, exploding in release against her own with a final groan.

He collapsed beside her, and she curled up against him, falling into a sated slumber.

Chapter Eight

Chase

He wasn't sure how much time had passed as he watched her sleeping form. Silken strands of honey splayed across his arm, her soft skin against his, the vision of a goddess, *his* goddess. He sensed during their first kiss, on the stairs at the safe-house, she hid something, and when he caught her dancing, unaware of his presence, still never would have guessed. A delicate balance of fire and ice lay against him, and he wanted to play with fire.

As he ran his fingers through those strands, he fought the urge for another go. Being so late, and given all the stress she endured, she needed the rest. With effort he arose, ignoring the pull of fatigue. There were people to track down.

Things weren't looking good. For the longest time names were coming up blank. No address, numbers, nothing. He'd probably have to reach out to the resources Mercer had offered after all. He'd all but given up when he stumbled on one that seemed familiar. On a hunch he checked it against the employee database of the facility housing Aiden. Bingo. He ran to his pants and grabbed the phone from the pocket.

"Agent Averey. What's the skinny?"

"I found a name for you. Scott Hunter. May be Aiden's mole. Need more to go on for the others. Maybe start with unreleased criminal records."

"Good job. We've uncovered more from the laptop and will have something for you tomorrow. Might help your work."

"Thank you, Sir."

"Great. Now get some sleep. I don't need one of my best agents getting sloppy."

"Understood, Sir."

All too happy to comply, he crawled beneath the thick blue comforter, throwing it over Cassidy as he curled up beside her. Hard to believe that angelic face concealed such wicked promises. All the times he worried she'd be another jealous type, she feared he only wanted to use her. He chuckled at the thought. The more he learned about her, the more she blew him away.

He'd no sooner leave or cheat on her than he would cut off his own limbs. A lifetime with her seemed far more appealing than what life he'd led before. As he nodded off, dreams of her infiltrated his mind, and the things they had yet to do.

Chapter Nine

Cassidy

Cassidy awoke with a start, slivers of sunlight penetrated the blinds, burning her eyes. She checked the alarm clock. Half past ten. Groggily she searched for her ringing phone, found it on the floor at the foot of the bed. Her body protested separation from Chase's warmth, goosebumps formed on her skin.

"Hello?"

"Sorry to wake you. Miss Macayla?"

"Speaking."

"This is Officer Langston from the Portland Police Department. We've received a report that your house got broken into. Your neighbors tell me you were away at the time of the incident, but two people abducted from the premises. Given the nature of the scene, and the fact that Stephen Melanson has escaped from prison, we need you to come in and answer some questions."

She was aware it had nothing to do with Steve, but didn't want to get into that, especially after Chase and Mercer's reaction to FBI involvement. They'd probably see this as something else to get in the way.

"When do I need to be there?"

"As soon as possible."

"I'm on my way."

"Very good. See you shortly."

Chase sat up.

"What was that about?" The sleepy drone of his voice was enough to make her want to jump him.

If she got to hear and see that every morning, she'd never leave the bed first.

"The police department wants to question me about the break-in yesterday, and about Steve."

"Be careful. Should trade your car in for another. If they're keen on finding you, it's only a matter of time before they do."

It was a miracle Tony and his goons never got a hold of her car. She assumed they recognized it belonged to her, but when Chase drove back to the store a couple of days after the incident, it was still there, unharmed. What were the odds of it not getting towed? The black Charger was one of the few expensive things of her mother's that hadn't tasted damage or destruction, as if protected by sheer luck. Could she really part with that?

"I don't know, maybe just get a paint job. Red might be nice. For now, I'm fine with parking in the back."

His jaw tensed.

"I'll be fine. Who's dumb enough to try anything at a police station?"

Anxiety flared as she watched the stern expression of the middle-aged, sandy-haired officer from across his desk. His scrutinizing stare only worsened her nerves. After sitting for almost two hours, her eagerness to leave neared the breaking point.

"For the last time! No, I have no idea where Steve is!"

"No need to raise your voice, ma'am."

She growled in frustration.

"I've been here for nearly two hours, answered all your questions, several times. No, I don't have a clue why he lost his marbles, I have no idea why anyone would bust him out, and I don't get why he'd abduct my brother. I don't understand any of this, and wish he'd just leave me the hell alone!"

The officer narrowed his eyes.

"Has anyone checked you for weapons?"

She crossed her arms, leaned back.

"I'm frustrated and angry, not trigger happy. I'd say given the circumstances, that should be understandable. And yes, I do have my permit."

"Doesn't anyone do their job around here?" He mumbled, running a hand down his face. He huffed in annoyance. "I'll let that slide because you haven't drawn your weapon out, but keep your tone respectful, or you won't get to keep it."

"Fine."

"Do you want to file a missing persons report?"

"Yes, for both."

"When we recapture Mister Melanson, can we still count on your testimony?"

"Of course."

"Alright. If anything else happens, or if he contacts you, let us know."

"I will."

"Thank you. You're free to go."

She adjusted her soft pink shirt over her blue jeans as she stood.

"Thank you."

Exiting the bustling brick building into the crowded lot, she froze. Someone had slashed the tires on her car. On approach she spied a folded piece of paper on the windshield, tucked beneath a wiper-blade. Perhaps Chase was right.

You can't get rid of me that easily. I'll be watching. At some point, I will catch you alone.

This was Steve's handwriting. No mistake. Adrenaline pumping, she snapped pictures of the tires with her cell, then rushed back inside. She struggled to catch her breath when she found the same man who questioned her moments before.

"What is it?"

She handed him the note.

"He left this on my car."

The man examined the page carefully.

"Anything else?"

"Yeah, he slashed my tires." She showed him the pictures on the phone.

"Come with me."

After having the photos from her phone copied, the car inspected and towed, and she answered more questions, she hopped a cab to the nearest car rental agency. It would be days before she'd get a call back from the mechanic. At least this time, nobody should recognize the car. Red was the next best color to black when it came to vehicles.

She couldn't walk into the motel fast enough. Chase wasn't there. Must have had something important to do. A hot shower was tempting. First things first, she needed the loo. To her dismay, as she finished up, something caught her eye. Blood rushed from her face.

A piece of plastic rested on the tissue. *Oh no...*

If only she didn't have an adverse reaction to the pill. Most women could take it, but not her. No, she had to be the one in however many that developed hypertension and nearly had a stroke.

Having been diagnosed with PCOS, her doctor told her she'd never have children, and if she did, she'd be lucky. Inside, she knew nothing was a hundred percent. It had taken a lot of hard work, exercise, and a healthy diet to manage her problems, along with natural supplementation and progesterone cream. Of all the negative symptoms she had to deal with, hide, the only plus was her above average strength. She liked being underestimated. Fear manifested deep.

What about last time? Did it break then too? Might she be pregnant? What would Chase say? What would he do? Her lungs seized. While she considered carrying his child to be an honor, she wasn't sure he even wanted one. No matter the outcome, she wouldn't abort it, she couldn't. The only time she'd ever kill something would be to protect herself or others.

Hurriedly she made way to the nearest pharmacy. Given her condition affected her hormones, how many tests did it take to be sure? Two? Three? She wasn't opposed to children, assuming herself able to have any, but this was the worst time to carry one. A pack of Trojans, a bar of dark chocolate, two First Response and one Clearblue Digital later, she approached the checkout counter.

The gray-haired woman smiled at her. At least the place was nearly dead.

"So, you're expecting?"

"Not sure." She smiled nervously.

How the hell was that any of her business? All the cashiers in the world and she got the slowest one with no filter for questions. She fidgeted, eager to leave.

"Children are such blessings, don't you know?"

She merely smiled and nodded.

Once paid, the woman handed her the purchases.

"Have a good day."

"Thanks, you too." How she managed not to snap eluded her.

Her mind raced as she hastened back to the motel. About three weeks, close to four. That's how long ago it happened. So preoccupied she was with everything it didn't occur to her to pay attention to her cycle.

How could this have happened? In the few relationships she had, this had never been an issue. Pleasure devices were a big help. After parking, her feet hastened to the bathroom. There wasn't much, but enough for the tests to be effective. She set them on the counter next to the sink and waited.

One pair of pink lines, another pair of pink lines, and a one to two weeks. Marc's sister used the same test and repeated what her doctor apparently said. The calculations on the Clearblue were always off from the doctors' diagnosis because of differing opinions of when the pregnancy actually begins. Her doctor diagnosed her as about two weeks further ahead.

No question, that first condom broke too. Quickly she ran to the bedroom, emptied the bag onto the bed, and tossed in the used tests. She stared at the condoms resting on top of the comforter. Useless purchase at this point, but non-refundable. She dashed to the lobby and tossed the used tests in the trash.

Eventually she'd tell him, she had to, but not until she gauged his reaction to the idea. In every scenario she pictured, it didn't end well. Assuming it would carry to term. Another risk associated with her condition. The doctor told her if she ever ended up pregnant, stress avoidance would be a high priority.

Chapter Ten

Chase

Meeting with one of Mercer's contacts certainly proved useful. An investigation on Scott was underway, the trap set. Time to catch a rat. If only he could figure out where Tony was staying. They might finally finish this, or find out who sat at the top.

He marched into the motel. Something about Cassidy's face as she stared at the television troubled him.

"You OK?"

She peered up in surprise as if she hadn't heard him enter.

"Yeah, I'm fine." Every instinct told him otherwise.

"What happened?" She considered her words.

"While at the station, Steve slashed my tires. My car's out right now for four replacements and a paint job."

He shook his head in disbelief.

"At least now you have the sense to do something. While you're at it, you really ought to change your plates. Those are a dead give away."

She nodded, a distant look in her eyes.

"You're right. I'll do that as soon as I can."

"How did you get here?"

"I rented a car. It's parked out back." She shook her head in dismay. "If not for what my mother left me, I'd be so screwed right now."

"Be careful what you spend. Use cash, not cards, they leave a trail for anyone wanting to track you down." Another nod of acknowledgment.

He removed his shirt, tossed it on the bed. In one fluid motion he moved beside her, wrapped his arm around her. She tensed at first, then relaxed against him.

"Something else bothering you?"

She smiled weakly.

"Nah, just starved. Wanted to wait 'til you got back to decide what to eat."

"Alright. How about Leonardo's Pizza?" That brought a smile to her lips.

"A pizza company with the same name as one of the ninja turtles? How cute. Should have named it Michaelangelo's. Better fit."

"That OK?"

"Yeah, whatever pizza you want, with a Greek salad."

About forty minutes later he opened the door to a bored looking young man with spiked midnight black hair and pale skin.

"One medium Nicole's Bacon Cheeseburger Paradise and a large Greek Salad?"

"Yep." Chase handed over the money, along with a fair tip.

"Thank you, sir."

The aroma stole into his nostrils. He closed the door and carried the items hurriedly, placing them on the bed before the pizza burned his arm.

"It smells delicious." Cassidy smiled.

Something about it seemed forced. Perhaps she worried for her brother. He admired her efforts to be strong when other people would probably have done something regrettable.

She leaned against him, digging the utensils and napkins out of the brown paper bag housing the salad container. Her hair brushed against his neck and shoulders, a floral scent wafted into his nostrils, setting his hunger on something other than food.

"We'll split the salad, OK?"

"Sounds good to me, I'll be sure to save room for dessert."

When she spun to face him he crushed her mouth with his. He'd waited all day to taste those lips, touch that body. For all he cared, pizza could wait. She nipped his lower lip.

"And you call me greedy." She giggled before taking out a slice and taking a bite.

"Mmm. Delicious." Her eyes closed as she delighted in the flavorful food as though an orgasm exploded in her mouth.

Little minx.

"What are you trying to do to me, woman?"

He watched her nip her lower lip, offering a mock innocent smile. He wanted fire, he got it.

"Nothing..."

Little tease.

"You're naughty."

She grinned deviously.

"I know."

He'd just sunk his teeth into a slice when his cell went off.

"Hello?"

"Something else for you, agent." Mercer spoke frankly.

"Shoot."

"Fort Gorges. Nineteen-hundred hours."

"That's only accessible by boat, Sir."

"You'll get a way there. There'll be a lobster boat waiting."

"Understood, Sir."

A frown formed on Cassidy's face.

"We can still eat together. Only, dessert will have to wait."

Taking in the way that pink shirt fit her form, cut low enough to frame a perfect pair of breasts, and how her jeans hugged her hips, his body was eager for the night.

"Oh Chase, you're such a tease. Should I start tallying your broken promises already?" Her words may have sounded like a warning, but held none of the bite.

She was disappointed, but contained herself and instead, leaned over and kissed him.

"I promised to save your brother, and I will, but I need to find out where they're hiding him."

Only then did he pick up on the worry veiled behind her eyes, mixed with something else. Fear?

"I know. I trust you."

He ate hurriedly, they spoke little. There was no shaking the feeling something else weighed on her mind. He prepped quickly, changing to his dark camo, and leaned in to kiss her before taking off.

"Chase..." She called as he opened the door.

"Yeah?" She hesitated.

"Be careful, please! I... I just... I need you to be careful." There was something cryptic behind those words.

"I'll be back. Don't worry about me, I can take care of myself."

"I know."

Whatever the issue, he'd deal with it later. He closed the door and drove to the pier, hopped on the boat, and arrived with enough time to set up the surveillance equipment and find a good place to use for cover. As he awaited their arrival, his mind wandered.

Given, Cassidy feared for her brother, her friend. Also, grieving took time. The concern etched in her features spoke of something different, other than Tony and Steve. The more he thought, the more confusion festered. She'd never tensed against him before, at least, not since they got together. Might it have something to do with him? Sounds from the area below stole his attention.

Tony and his beefed up entourage meeting another shady group in an isolated area by the docks. All had hands hovering over holstered weapons. He adjusted his head piece, plugged in the USB, and listened, squatting lower in the overhead brush.

Clouds hung overcast, threatening rain, darkening the already dimming daylight. A slow, cool breeze chilled his bones, but he refused to move a muscle.

"Got the supply?" A hooded man with a scar running across his cheek approached Tony, briefcase in hand.

"It's on-board." The scarred man pointed his thumb in the direction of a large fishing boat. "Don't know why we don't just do this at your headquarters."

"Because one can never be too careful. I don't need vultures in my roost, especially when I've got two pigeons in a cage."

"Right." He handed Tony the briefcase. "The info on those artifacts you requested. Make up your mind quick. We may have another interested buyer."

He needed to find Tony's headquarters. Two pigeons? Were Cassidy's brother and friend captive there? Tony pulled a massive envelope from inside his dark blue hooded jacket and handed it over.

"Here's the funds. I'll get back to you by five tomorrow for the artifacts. I have to run it by my client."

"Have you retrieved any more info from the homeland security database?"

Tony took a quick look around to ensure they were alone.

"They're planning to send agents to Saudi Arabia to investigate some connections with cells here in the States. Can't find anything on the military, ever since Aiden got captured." Venom oozed from his mouth at the mention of his brother's capture. "Something's going on, and I can't access certain areas of their system that I had previously been able to."

Good to see the Sergeant Major was keeping up. The scar-faced man laughed.

"Let me guess, their password used to be 'password' before someone grew a brain cell and changed it?"

"Fuck you, Rick. My hacking skills have gotten your boss further ahead than he ever imagined. His weapons sales have skyrocketed. I'll find out what their plans are. It's only a matter of time."

Chase grinned. He had Tony admitting to being a hacker. Now if only he could figure out where Tony's headquarters was located. Thunder clasped overhead as it started to rain.

"Let's get this over with. Quick, transfer this shit and let's go." Rick, the scar-faced man, rushed.

He watched them transfer the cargo. They had a lot more than he assumed could fit on the boat, yet they managed. By his estimations, it had to be at least a twenty-five million dollar street value. The net was closing fast on Tony and his men if only he could get those hostages released. He needed a way to track Tony. Impossible at the moment. All things in due time, for Cassidy's sake, he hoped it wouldn't be too late.

Chapter Eleven

Cassidy

What to do... How could she tell Chase? Staring at the television screen while the same news reporter as before babbled on about Steve still being at large didn't help her anxiety. Chase was a reasonable man, he'd understand it wasn't her fault, wouldn't he? That she'd never stray. These things happened.

Knowing she had to tell him such life changing news had her anxiety threatening to take over. She kept reminding herself that Chase was smart, understanding. Surely he'd know she wouldn't do anything mean spirited. She'd figure out her words, tell him in the morning, after a night's sleep her mind might better be able to find the right way to tell him.

The doorknob rattling startled her. A soaking wet Chase came in from the darkness outside, the way his black camo attire clung to him had her wanting to peel the fabric off and then some. He dropped his duffel bag on the floor, squatted down, opened it up, and rummaged through its contents.

"Mind giving me a hand, or are you just going to lay there undressing me with your eyes?"

"I can use more than just my eyes if you'd like."

He paused, darkened gaze taking her in. Not two seconds and he pinned her to the bed, drawing a squeal from her. His wet clothes dampened hers as he straddled her. So close, the combined scent of earth, woods, and man left a tilt a whirl spinning in her stomach.

"I suppose it can wait a little."

"I think you should take off your clothes before you catch a cold. Or you could let me."

Chase flung off his sopping wet clothing and plopped them on the floor before easing her out of hers.

"All better?" Her teeth sunk into her lower lip as the dampness of the rain glistened over his skin.

"Uh-huh."

Leaning over, he bit gently at her ear, making her shiver. His mouth made its way past her jaw, tongue trailing liquid fire down her neck as he released her wrists. Hands caressed her body, a slow exploration, focusing on the hardened peaks of her breasts. She arched against him with a moan, nails biting his biceps.

It wasn't long before he had her writhing beneath him, panting. He seemed determined to take his time, leaving her insides weeping for release.

"Oh Chase, please stop teasing me!" She breathed.

His wicked grin left her insides a jumbled mess.

"It's worth the wait." The way he rasped his dark promise in that deep rich voice had her ready to blow.

By the time a hand reached the moistened nub at the vee of her hips she couldn't take it anymore.

"Chase, *please*!" She pleaded.

He smirked. His fingers infiltrated her core mercilessly, her hips moved in welcome as he sent her spiraling toward rapture with moans of ecstasy. Withdrawal left her whimpering in protest.

Chase reached for the drawer of the nightstand, opened the drawer, pulled out the unopened box of Trojans. His brows burrowed.

"These aren't the condoms I brought."

Anxiety threatened to mount.

"I bought them today. Thought we could use them."

He smiled.

"You think of everything, don't you?"

"I try." She managed a smile.

With no time wasted he had one out and on, then claimed her with a groan that threatened to send her over the edge. No gentleness remained as he flipped her over onto her knees and hammered into her, grabbing a fistful of hair and pulling back, sending her flying into delicious oblivion. He turned her face toward him, his mouth crushed hers, capturing her pleasured cries as he gave a few final shuddered thrusts.

Collapsing to her side, he tossed the used rubber in the trash can in the corner beside the nightstand.

"You're an awful tease." She chided.

He feigned insult.

"Who, me? Never!"

Cassidy threw on her clothes and headed to the washroom, stomach unusually queasy. She must have looked off because Chase's expression became one of concern.

"You alright?"

"Just a little queasy." Her stomach churned another wave.

Had to be morning sickness. When it hit, why did it not only happen in the mornings? Hand on her stomach, she rushed to the washroom.

"Cassidy?"

A few minutes of heaving and she wiped her mouth with some tissue. Pizza didn't look or taste so appetizing on the way out. Chase came to check on her, eyes burning a hole in the back of her head. With effort she turned, leaned her head against the wall.

Marc's sister dealt with this for three months, starting around the same time. How did she manage? As she peered up Chase waved the receipt in front of her. *Oh shit...* Must have forgotten it on the bed.

"Care to explain why you'd waste money on *three* pregnancy tests?"

She sighed despairingly. *Here goes...*

"Because I'm pregnant." As his face reddened, she cast her gaze downward.

"Christ! Look at me!" Reluctantly she obeyed. "Seeing how I've used a condom every fucking time, I know it's not mine, so don't fucking try to tell me it is! Got over my apparent death pretty quickly, didn't you?"

She gaped, terror engulfed her. Without even asking her side, he'd already concluded the worst. Hadn't she proven herself? After he'd cracked her shell, drew her out, taken her heart, he determined to render it no more than ashes.

Her breathing ceased. Pain coiled around her heart. He clearly didn't know her at all.

"There's been nobody, only you. The condom broke, they both did." Striving for calm proved difficult.

"Lying bitch! You're just like Rachel. A manipulative, good-for-nothing whore. How long have you been hiding this from me?" He seethed.

Her vision blurred as tears seared a path down her face. This couldn't be happening. She rose quickly, circling around him and backing out of the bathroom. His eyes, the way they bore into hers, screamed danger, like he'd just deemed her his worst enemy. She shuddered fearfully.

"I only found out today, and I'm not Rachel!" All that came out was a hoarse whisper.

"You're right, you're worse! At least she wasn't stupid enough to get knocked up!"

Quickly her resolve was slipping. To keep from doing or saying something she'd regret appeared inevitable. In seconds she had her sneakers on.
It went beyond her worst fears. She put on her belt and strapped on her weapons.

"I didn't plan this, and I didn't sleep with anyone else! The condom broke, that's it!"

He ripped the alarm clock from the plug-in and whipped it with a loud roar. She ducked out of the way as it crashed against the wall near her head. Flashbacks of her father, throwing furniture, screaming, veins throbbing as he beat her mother, brother, her. His violent temper had even caused her mother to miscarry. She placed a hand over her stomach protectively.

No, she wouldn't make the same mistake her mother did, she was stronger than that. Chase stormed toward her, every inch of his skin deep crimson, fists balled tight, face menacing. Every scenario like this always ended the same way, with her getting bruises, sometimes bleeding, and Chase was conditioned to kill.

"Stop!" She raised her hands defensively, backing away as he drew closer.

He continued on, not heeding her plea. Backed against the wall, she let her shaky hand hover over the knife at her side.

"Please, stop!" It was near impossible to focus, between the blurred vision caused by tears and her body's uncontrollable trembling.

She didn't want to. The idea of hurting him killed her, but if it came to protecting herself, she would, if left with no other choice. Although, something inside told her that by taking it out, she'd merely be providing him with a weapon. To her amazement and relief, he did, with a sneer.

"You going to stab me?"

She felt for the door handle, never taking her eyes off him.

"You whipped an alarm clock at my head, and you're raging like the Hulk, coming at me like you're going to attack me! Y - you're scaring me!"

His laugh resonated, cold enough to extinguished the fires of hell.

"Oh please, you want to play the victim now? I have to say, you really had me going for a while. You have a way with people, but really, you're a fucking joke! You'd make a great crooked salesman, err, woman!" She gasped in shock and dismay.

Who was this person standing before her, like a complete stranger with Chase's voice and body? Not a hint of the kind, reasonable man she knew, the one that stole her heart so many years ago. She was speechless. Her lungs burned, unable to draw air.

"You think I want to lay a hand on you? I can't even stand looking at you right now, let alone the idea of touching you! You're a fucking whore, and I'm so done with you!" Her heart shattered into a million pieces.

It truly was one of her worst nightmares come to life. Finding the knob she opened the door.

"I can't believe you, Chase! I - I thought you had more sense than this!"
She croaked.

It took every ounce of effort not to openly compare him to her father.

He opened his mouth to speak as she slammed the door behind her. In less
than a minute she exited the parking lot and raced down the highway. She felt
every inch an idiot. How did she ever think him a decent person?

Her mind returned to the times she stuck up for him, protected him. All the
moments with him that meant the world to her. What the hell happened? Pain and
fear gripped her heart and squeezed. With one hand she wiped at the torrent
pouring down her face. In that moment, he'd gone from making her feel safest with
him to the deepest sense of danger. The coldest chill coursed through her spine.

What would she do about her brother, and Sheila? They remained trapped
somewhere, prisoners of Aiden's brother. There had to be a way to get them back
without involving Chase, but she wasn't exactly Nancy Drew.

There also remained the newfound issue. How had he managed to hide
such a cold, heartless nature? He didn't even give her a chance. Surely better to
find out sooner rather than later, but never would be better. She really hoped this
kid didn't have a temper, or she'd be in trouble. Another lesson learned too late.
With no idea where else to go, she drove home.

Still a disaster, surrounded by yellow tape. She parked out front,
approached, and examined the building, ignoring the pouring rain. For the longest
time she wandered the interior aimlessly, shivering from the chill in the damp air.

With this house, she could give her child a home. The mortgage cleared
when the life insurance paid out, so if she did things intelligently, they'd have a
decent life. Thoughts of Chase clawed at her heart once more, she tried to push

them aside. He made up his mind about her, nothing she could do. No amount of logic would penetrate in his current state of mind.

She found it impossible to sleep under that roof in its current condition. The scene left a lingering uneasiness, like eyes following her every move. Unable to handle anymore, she walked briskly to the rental, hopped in, and drove.

Cranking up the radio, Camila and Machine Gun Kelly belted a duet, something about bad things. If only Chase would make an effort to understand her, but he didn't even care to try, determined that his was the only correct way of thinking, that only he could be right. All of a sudden, she became nothing to him.

It was a long drive before she found a hotel. Bright lights inside and out, packed parking lot, nothing out of place. Looked expensive, safe, the best place to go. The only parking spots available were at the back, in the darkest area of the lot. She didn't worry about her appearance, or attempt to fix the hair matted to her face. All she wanted was a safe-haven. Summoning what little bravado remained, she entered, looking nervously about.

"Oh, you poor thing!" A graying woman at the admissions desk exclaimed.

"Do you have a room?" Cassidy mumbled, teeth chattering.

The sympathetic woman checked the computer before her.

"Yes, you're in luck, someone canceled last minute. You can stay in the honeymoon suite."

Oh just kill me now...

"I'll take it."

"How long will you be staying?" She had no idea what to say. "It's available for a week."

"Just the night, thanks." She'd have to figure out what to do after a decent rest.

Seconds after presenting her credit card, the woman had it swiped and returned, along with the key card for the room.

"It's on the fourth floor, room 436. Would you like someone to help you with any luggage?"

"No." Cassidy shook her head. "I can manage, thank you."

The woman gave the standard 'thank you' spiel but her mind wandered elsewhere. What would she do until the house got repaired? They'd told her when she called earlier, it would be at least a month. She forced herself to focus. First things first, new clothes, and a shower.

After perusing a few of the clothing shops inside the hotel she settled on a couple of form flattering button-up blouses, a couple of pairs of jeans, and a few lacy bras and panties.

She had no trouble finding the room and was in awe after stepping inside. King size bed covered by a beautiful blue comforter, polished wooden furniture, leather couch, massive wall-mounted TV, even a jacuzzi. Over the bed hung an over-sized mirror. The bathroom housed a stand-alone shower, extra-large bathtub, and a sensor-operated toilet. Incredible.

The shampoo and conditioner provided by the hotel smelled amazing, like a rain-forest in a bottle. After dropping her bag of clothes just outside the bathroom door, she plugged in the stopper, ran the water as hot as tolerable, then slunk in the enormous tub.

Sinking deep, she let the heat ease into her cold bones. Her mind wandered. Did doctor Hartman do prenatal? What would she do if the pregnancy did go well? How did one explain to a child that its father didn't even want to acknowledge it as his? A whore, crooked saleswoman, that's what he said, what he called her. She fought the moisture in her eyes that threatened another torrent.

The child would know a hard working, loving mother who put family first. One who sacrificed everything to give it the best life possible. No man would interfere with that, and if she did find somebody down the road, he'd have to be a good man and father material, nothing less. Never did she want a child of hers to know a measure of the suffering she endured growing up. If she ever found herself in a similar situation, she'd probably want to do the same thing her mother tried to do.

Washed and dried, she dressed quickly. Her stomach rumbled. Peering out the wall length window next to the bed, lights on the sign attached to the building next door caught her eye. A restaurant. Worth a try.

Half way across the lot a familiar voice fed terror into her spine.

"Finally. Tony sends his regards."

She spun around quickly. After a moment she recognized him. Steve! Only with a black goatee and shaved head, clad in leather and jeans. He appeared eerily calm.

"How did you get out?" He aimed a pistol at her.

"Tony. Gave me a job and some resources so I can keep an eye on you. You've been elusive, but I figured you'd go back to that house eventually, so I've been patrolling the street. When I saw you, I followed you here."

Pulling her gun quickly, she aimed at him.

"I wouldn't do that if I were you. The smartest thing for you to do is come with me. I'll bring you to your brother. Joe, is it? And Sheila?"

Ice coursed through her veins. If they got her, they'd kill her, and it wasn't just her now.

"No, tell me where they are!" She pointed between his eyes.

He snickered, tightening his finger around the trigger.

"No dice."

She barely dodged behind a car before his gun went off. The air crackled as it discharged. A quick scan of the lot left her discouraged. The fenced in parking lot only had one way in or out, and a vehicle blocked the exit.

"There are only two ways out of here, Cassidy. Either with me, or in a body-bag."

Crouching low and creeping between vehicles, she pulled the cell from her pocket and dialed 911.

Chapter Twelve

Chase

As he waited impatiently for the Sergeant Major, thoughts raced through his head. How could he have misjudged her so badly? Flames of rage still burned his body. Clearly she'd played him, stabbed him in the back just like everyone else. How stupid of him to consider her as innocent as she appeared. How had he not seen it? He slammed the garbage can against the wall, watching the contents fly out.

Both rubbers caught his eye. Unsure why, perhaps it was his investigative nature, he went to examine them. The one she bought appeared thicker, completely intact. He picked up the one from the pack he carried, studied it carefully. The end was missing. Pinched off, not smooth like a cut, or punctured, but like something ripped it off at the end.

He picked up the receipt, checked the date. She'd told the truth. His blood chilled. Where were the tests? He searched every inch of the place, but found nothing. Where would she hide them?

He rushed outside and ran to the small lobby at the end of the building. Vacant, good. He checked the garbage, spied a pharmacy bag. Quickly he grabbed it and ran back to the room, grateful the rain had slowed. Emptying the contents on the bed, he collapsed to his knees.

Three pregnancy tests, all positive. One said one to two weeks. Before he could give it much consideration a loud banging on the door stole his attention. He got up and answered. Mercer, with a stunned expression on his face as he took in the sight of the room.

"What happened? It looks like a fight broke out." Before he found the ability to answer, Mercer spied the tests on the bed.

"You aware that those are two weeks off from doctor diagnosis? So one to two weeks would more accurately be three to four. Found out when my wife had her third." He face-palmed hard as his heart dropped.

The safe-house... Cassidy told the truth, about everything. He ran his hands over his head, over and over. Like a fool he refused to listen, suspecting the worst after what Rachel had done to him, and Aiden. He just assumed he was right, that Cassidy had blind-sighted him as well, but she hadn't. No, she'd proven herself true after all. As the words he'd spoken to her, called her, flooded him, his heart bled. He felt so sure he was right, didn't see any other way, and it may have just cost him.

He fucked up, worse than he ever had. What's worse, he let her run right out the door, pregnant with *his* child, and her life on the line. There had to be a way to find her. Hopefully she'd forgive him. If so, he'd do anything to make it up to her.

Just remembering the expression on her face as her hand hovered over her knife. Was that the same one she had looking at her father during the times he got physical? If so, he must have come across as a monster. His chest constricted painfully. He'd done that to her, knowing what she'd dealt with, and while pregnant. He gritted his teeth.

While he didn't plan on fatherhood for a long time yet, he'd do the honorable thing. He'd not shirk his responsibilities. Chase swallowed hard. After how he dealt with her, he'd be lucky if she ever spoke to him again.

"I need to find Cassidy."

"Explain yourself, agent." It came out edged with annoyance.

"She's missing... and pregnant." Mercer's face turned the deepest shade of red he'd ever seen.

"Christ's sakes, Averey! You sure bring FUBAR to a whole new level!"

"Yeah..."

"Do you have any idea where she might be?"

He could only guess. Her home remained uninhabitable, and she had nobody to stay with. Either she slept in her car, a hotel, or motel. Or ended up in the hospital, or in Tony's clutches...

Mercer fiddled around on his cell. Voices, both male and female, came through.

"Let's see if she's at a hotel or motel. We can track if there are any credit card purchases under her name in the area."

Mercer held a hand up for silence.

"Don't bother. I've got a location. We need to hurry."

Several police cruisers dotted the lot of the extravagant hotel. Unable to see her, he jumped from Mercer's vehicle and ran for the entrance. Not in the grand lobby either. He approached the administration desk. A graying woman greeted him.

"I'm looking for Cassidy Macayla. Would you please tell me where she is?" The woman's gentle eyes turned wary.

"Given the circumstances especially, I can't release any information about potential guests."

He growled in frustration.

"Forget it. I'll find her myself, if I have to knock on every door."

"You'd do that with several cop cars out there?"

"That's my girlfriend, I have to find her!" She glared daggers.

"What kind of boyfriend leaves his girlfriend like that?"

The heat of embarrassment flooded him. His shoulders slumped.

"An imperfect one who made a big mistake." He gulped.

After a lengthy assessment of him, her stance softened slightly.

"I used to be an interrogator for the police department. Years ago, but I can still tell when someone's lying."

He grinned.

"No kidding." Her tone remained serious.

"Not kidding. She's in room 436. The flower shop's still open for another twenty minutes if you need anything."

He subdued the urge to tell her to butt out.

"Got it, thanks."

Would she even take flowers? Some women didn't, some preferred chocolates, or stuffed animals, or none of those. He bypassed the flower shop and went up to the room. Before he could knock, an officer opened the door.

"When we find him, we'll do everything possible to make sure he doesn't get out again."

"Thank you, officer Brody."

He didn't like the way the officer looked at her, with a full body scan and expression that said he'd lay it to her right then and there if possible. Taking in the sight of her button up pale blue blouse that framed her chest perfectly, the hint of black lace beneath, and the snug fitting jeans, he understood. A vision, with a halo of silken strands framing the sides of her breasts. Her delicate fingers poked out of the sleeves as she uncrossed her arms. His jeans tightened, he coughed.

"Excuse me." The cop said curtly as he took off down the hall.

Chase stepped in, closing the door behind him. The room was impressive. Her expression froze him in his tracks.

"What are you doing here? I thought you were done with me." Her tone bled ice.

She crossed her arms and sat on the bed. At least she spoke to him. A promising start.

"I let my past and fears get the better of me. I've dealt with a lot, perhaps it's all taken a tole on me. What you said about the condoms breaking... The way it happened, I didn't think it possible."

Her eyes narrowed.

"You actually checked the condoms?" She huffed. "After everything we've been through, my word should suffice. Never-mind our friendship before that. I'm not perfect, I recognize that I make mistakes, but I'd never do the things you accused me of. I think I felt the way my mother must have." Her voice grew distant.

She turned to him, eyes hardened.

"My mother had a miscarriage because of him. Nearly died because of it."

He sat beside her. The man truly did qualify for extinction. She stiffened.

"I wasn't going to hit you, I'd never do that! But I was furious. I thought you cheated on me. Couldn't see any other way. I found your tests, and the Sarge told me about the week count discrepancy. It's really mine?"

She growled.

"Yes it's yours! You really don't know me, do you? I'm not the type to sleep around. If I don't to do flings or one night stands, why would I? Not only that, I've wanted you since we were teens. Why would I *ever* want to screw that up? God! I'm the type of person that turns down a free pass!"

His eyes bugged out, recalling her revelation of more of her surprises. What enigma of a woman sat beside him?

"You turned down sleeping with other men, even though he did as he pleased with other women? Why didn't you look me up?" She snorted.

"All the reasons I just mentioned. That's not my style. I just need one man to make me feel like a queen, and the idea of 'club hopping' doesn't appeal to me." She was just full of surprises.

Cassidy swallowed with a frown.

"You said some pretty harsh things and scared me near to death. I thought you knew me better than that, that I'd never deliberately make you angry, hurt, or undermine you. I'm not sure what to think now, I've never heard you speak, or seen you behave that way before. It's like I've met a completely different person. You'd rather cut me out completely than understand me, or acknowledge that you might be wrong. Never before did I think you would hurt me. I'm not your enemy, Chase. Until you realize that... I don't know..."

"I didn't mean to." She sighed.

"If I give you another chance, you have to realize I'm not your enemy. You can't treat me like one every time something happens that you don't understand, or can't control, or if I don't agree with you on something. We'll have disagreements, it doesn't mean I'm against you." She gulped nervously.

"I also have a sense of duty and obligation, and I've spent my entire life cautious of words and deeds, constantly on my guard. Considering potential consequences, outcomes you can't fathom, because many I've had to deal with. Yet, I put myself, my heart, on the line for you. I opened up to you, let you in where only the rare person sees, stuck my neck out enough times that how I feel should be apparent. If that's not enough, then nothing ever will be."

"I'm sorry. I just couldn't see how you were telling the truth."

"At least you looked into it, eventually. I'll give you the benefit of the doubt *this time*, but you can't keep doing that, or it won't work."

He threw his arms around her. Unbelievable. She actually forgave him! She returned the hug, and he pressed his mouth to hers, expressing all the appreciation within. After a long moment he released her.

"You know, your own knife can be used against you in a fight. Mind if I teach you something?"

She smiled.

"Sure." They stood.

"When you are in a fight, a knife requires you to be close to your opponent in order to use it, which is a disadvantage. Your attacker can either disarm you or use it against you." He took her arm to demonstrate, bending it and moving her hand toward her side in a stabbing motion. "They can also try to disarm you." He quickly scanned the room. "Hold on a second."

After searching the room in a rush he found a small information booklet in the drawer of the nightstand.

"Here, hold this."

She nodded and once it was in her hand, in one swift movement, he performed his well practiced move. To his amazement the book remained in her hand. Not even a slip. Her face turned quizzical. He blinked, then tried again, harder. Other than flinching, nothing. That usually worked well. How could that be? No way in hell would he admit his surprise. It took a moment to find the ability to speak.

"You must be doing that on purpose."

A confused expression greeted him as she rubbed her arm.

"That hurt! You're really nasty, you know that? You're lucky I love you, otherwise, I might have to slap you for that!" She continued to rub it a moment before rolling up her sleeve and giving a close examination, her voice nowhere near threatening.

Her eyes widened, but she said nothing more, merely pulled the sleeve back over her arm, and rubbed a moment longer. Suddenly, he was eager to get out of there. Good thing she wasn't short tempered or spiteful.

"Anyway, we need to go. This will be all over the news soon if it's not already. Don't want Tony finding you."

She hesitated.

"It's not just you now, and I'm not going to let anything happen to either of you." Another sigh loosed from her mouth.

"I guess. What about my brother?"

"I'll take care of it. Don't worry." She frowned, but said nothing.

He stood.

"You'll return your rental, I'll follow with the Sergeant. Then we'll drive you back to the motel. You're not leaving without me again." She rolled those sexy emerald green eyes as she stood.

Gathering her things she followed him out. When they got to the lobby, she returned her key card to the administration desk.

"I guess it's not the safest place for me, given what happened. So I've been given alternate arrangements. Sorry for all the trouble."

The woman assessed them a moment before letting her attention fall on Cassidy.

"You're no trouble at all, sweetheart. Let me take this opportunity to suggest joining our membership. It's free to join, and you get discounts on your stays." She gave Cassidy a pamphlet and a card which she stamped several squares. "Also, with this, every twelve nights you get one free. Only works if you're a member."

The way she glared at him told him she anticipated he'd drive Cassidy back to the hotel again. He gritted his teeth.

"Thank you! I'd like to join now, if that's OK." Cassidy's surprise was evident in her voice.

"Of course!"

It took all he had not to drag her out before she received her card.

"Your membership number works when booking online. Hope you come back soon." The woman offered Cassidy a sympathetic smile.

When Cassidy turned her back, he got greeted with a scowl. Sure, he deserved it, but she still should have kept it to herself. He wrapped his arm around Cassidy as they made way to Mercer's black Nissan.

"Miss Macayla. Glad you're alright. We're going to follow you as you return your rental."

"OK, thanks." The man gave a curt tilt of his head.

"Will see you shortly."

She sauntered to her rental and drove. They followed close.

"Did you get any Intel?"

Chase peered in the rear view mirror from the passenger side. So far, no vehicle behind them.

"Yeah, if you get a membership, you get discounts on your stay. After your twelfth, you get a free night."

"Agent..."

"Yeah, yeah. Melanson got away, police are still looking. No sign of the Feds."

"If we can get Melanson, we might be able to get info on Tony."

"I don't suppose that laptop has Tony's headquarters on it."

"Haven't found any addresses on it yet, but there are still files we need to unlock. We have reason to suspect their overseas contacts are in Saudi Arabia, but we're still working on their emails."

"How should we flush out Melanson?"

"Find someone to be Miss Macayla's doppelgänger. We'll figure it out."

"Understood, Sir."

One way or another, he'd keep his promise to her. He'd save her brother and bring Tony down, or die trying.

Chapter Thirteen

Cassidy

She was a sucker. No ifs, and's, or buts. Her mind and heart were at odds, but she'd give him the benefit of the doubt. After all, it was the first time since they met he got so angry, and she'd accidentally pissed him off before. About fifteen minutes later she parked the car and left the keys in the drop box before hopping in the back of Mercer's vehicle, a soothing voice coming through the speakers, pleading for someone not to kill the magic.

"Mind if I get a picture of you, Miss Macayla?"

Her brows furrowed in confusion. Why would the Sergeant want a picture of her?

"What for?"

"We want to capture Mister Melanson, but we'll need to draw him out, hopefully get some info on Tony, where his headquarters resides, maybe find out where your brother is at same time. Given your new found development, you won't be partaking in anymore risky endeavors."

"Why do you need a picture of me?"

"We're going to create your twin."

"I see. I don't have any pictures. You'll need to take one." Despite how far she'd come since her youth, she still didn't like her picture taken.

No matter how far she'd come, scars would always remain.

"At the motel. Need to take a few to get everything. Anything off and it won't work."

Her nerves flared. She didn't like this one bit, but if they could get anything out of him, if it would help her brother, did she really have a choice?

"Alright."

She didn't enjoy their little fashion shoot and video recording, it left her on edge, along with the terrifying state of the room upon arrival. They'd made haste cleaning up before starting. It took everything to resist the urge to grab the phone and hit delete. Doubtful they missed a single angle.

"That ought to do it." Mercer stated as he pocketed his phone.

"You sure this will help?"

"I don't employ amateurs." She crooked an eyebrow with a slight smirk. "Pretty sure you're not on the clock this time, Miss Macayla, but point taken."

"How long will this take?"

"There's no knowing for certain, but I already have someone in mind. Chase will need to help me since she has to not only look like you, but imitate your mannerisms."

"OK."

"We'll need what locations you frequent, starting with your mother's place." She flopped on the bed, mind racing.

"Well, I get my groceries at the Market on Somerset on Friday afternoons, at the end of the month I go to Apothecary By Design on Preble for natural supplements, supplies for health and wellness, and occasional prescriptions. Whatever I don't order online." It took a moment for her to realize Mercer was taking notes.

"I don't go out and do much for fun, so that's pretty unpredictable. All my workouts are currently being done at home, haven't been to a gym in months. Think it will still be some time before I can, given my current circumstances. I don't have a job right now, I think we all understand why." Mercer and Chase both coughed nervously as she gave them both a knowing look.

"I get most of my clothing and household items from the Salvation Army, also at the end of the month. Other things I get from Amazon, eBay, once in a while Craigslist. Not sure what else I can say that might be useful."

Mercer smiled with a nod.

"That'll be fine. Thank you, Miss Macayla."

"Alright." She stifled a yawn.

"Chase, meet me at my office tomorrow, thirteen hundred hours. We'll get started on this."

"Yes, Sir."

"Good." The Sergeant turned to Cassidy.

"Take care of yourself, Miss Macayla. If you need anything, give me a call."

"I'm OK, thank you." She smiled appreciatively.

With a sharp tilt of his chin, Mercer left. Cassidy flopped on her side, the pull of exhaustion overwhelming. Chase crawled in beside her, gently running his hands through her hair in silence. She figured him exhausted since his breathing soon slowed, rhythmic, before sleep finally claimed her.

Chase's phone going off woke her up, her queasy stomach had her making a b-line to the bathroom. What time was it? Her head remained in a haze of fatigue. Chase's low tone crept into her ears from the other room between bouts of heaving. He found her still hunched over the latrine when he entered.

"You alright?"

"Fine." She managed the word with difficulty.

When she had nothing left, she leaned against the wall, turning slowly. Chase's concerned expression greeted her. He buried his hands in his jean pockets, black shirt hanging loosely off his broad shoulders.

"How long is this supposed to go on?"

She shrugged.

"It depends. Usually about three months." He swore beneath his breath.

"I have to meet the Sergeant in an hour. Will you be OK?"

"I'll be fine." A weak smiled spread across her face.

"Can I get you anything while I'm out? Chicken salad?"

The idea of eating had her stomach churning again, but she couldn't just avoid food, even if it meant throwing up more.

"Sure, thanks."

"Anything to drink?"

"Ginger tea, if you can." A natural remedy to help with nausea.

Hopefully it worked on morning sickness too.

"I'll try to get some things for you, to help until it's safe to chance taking you to a doctor." She summoned the strength to chuckle.

"I'm pregnant, not dying. I'll be alright while things get sorted out." His doubt-filled expression made her nervous. "Really, it's OK. My purse is next to the bed, by the nightstand."

"That's OK, I got it."

"Chase..." He shook his head.

"No, I got it."

With a frown, she released a sigh of resignation.

"Alright."

With effort she stood, returned to the bed. She could sleep another hour, minimum.

"You look exhausted. Get some more sleep, I'll be back before you know it."

She rolled her eyes as she flopped on her back.

"Thank you for you concern. I'm fine, really."

"Did you just roll those pretty eyes at me?"

She snickered before narrowing her gaze on him, crooking a devious smile.

"Flattery will get you nowhere, *Mister Averey...*"

He stiffened, causing her smile to broaden.

"Right... If you're any better later I'll make sure you pay for that one, little minx."

A giggle bubbled up.

"We'll see."

With a wicked grin he left. She'd nearly fallen back to sleep when her phone rang.

"Hello?"

"Your car's ready. You can pick it up any time."

"Thanks. I'll stop by when I can."

"Alright. See you later."

Her phone went off again, this time a text message. Blood turned to ice in her veins.

Surprise...

A sharp series of knocks on the door set her panicked heart racing. She rushed to the peephole. *Steve!* Another message.

You really should have disabled the GPS on your phone.

In haste she reached for her gun, dialing Mercer's number while rushing to the bathroom. If he knew where she was, it was only a matter of time before Aiden's brother did as well, if he didn't already. Quickly she locked the door.

The Sergeant's voice graced her ears just as a loud crash echoed in the other room.

"It's Cassidy. Steve, err, Mister Melanson just broke into the motel."

The sound of rummaging and footsteps approaching, stopping at the bathroom door, left her shaken.

"I hear you moving around in there, Cassidy."

"Stall him as long as you can, Miss Macayla. Someone will be there to get him. I realize that might be asking a lot..."

"Yes, I'll... I'll do that." She whispered, then put down the phone.

With trembling arms she aimed as Steve busted through the door, shot his legs, sending him crumbling with a roar of pain. She pounced on him before he could steady his weapon, cracking the butt of her gun on his head, knocking him out.

In less than a minute she'd taken some ties from one of Chase's bags and secured Steve's hands behind his back, also binding his feet for good measure. She grabbed her phone.

"You still there?"

"Miss Macayla, everything alright?"

"I have him bound pretty good, he's out like a light."

"Excellent work."

"There's something not right about this. He doesn't have the knowledge to track my phone, yet he says he used it to find me here."

A long string of swears filled her ears.

"We'll deal with this, one thing at a time. Once we apprehend Mister Melanson, I will have you brought here and we can figure out another living arrangement. In the meantime, I want you to store what you can on Chase's laptop from your phone, then clear the memory, destroy it, and toss it in the trash."

"OK."

She hastened to do as Mercer instructed. Nearly everything got uploaded when pained groans reached her ears. Steve struggled to sit up.

"Bitch!" He seethed.

"Don't make me gag you too."

Before he could articulate a rebuttal, two massive, muscular men in black body armor, brandishing weapons, stormed the room.

"This him?" The taller of the two demanded gruffly.

"Yes."

Wordlessly they grabbed him, roughly dragging him out the door.

"We have another vehicle waiting for you, grab everything and put it in the trunk." In a rush she did all the Sergeant Major and the two men instructed before proceeding to the vehicle.

Entering Mercer's office after so long seemed surreal. The concern on both Chase and Mercer's face was fully apparent. She hastened to the seat next to Chase before the Sergeant Major's desk.

"Glad you got here safely." Mercer greeted with a smile.

"Thank you."

"Now Chase, you understand your mission?"

"Yes, Sir."

"Good. Be there for nineteen-hundred hours."

He turned to her as Chase stood.

"I'll meet you at the entrance." The words were a whisper as he left.

"As we speak everything you brought is being moved to Chase's vehicle. You'll need to replace your phone. I suggest changing the number."

Her mind raced. She still had to get her car. Perhaps she'd take Chase's advice and change the plates. The fear that Steve would only get out again was unshakable. Would his capture make things worse for Joe and Sheila? She shivered nervously and nodded.

"Alright. What's going to happen to him? Will he be able to escape again?"

"No, not this time. He's scheduled for placement in a maximum security prison. Won't be going anywhere this time."

The news should have left her some sense of relief, but instead she felt something worse awaited her.

"Thank you."

"What progress is being made in finding my brother? Will this make things worse for them?"

He pressed his lips in a thin line.

"We're doing what we can. If all goes well, we'll have a lead tonight. At the very least, in the next day or two." Not the answer she wanted.

This feeling of helplessness was reaching near breaking point but she bit her tongue. If only this danger, to her, to them, would finally pass. She prayed her brother was alright.

"Thank you." She rose to leave.

"Don't lose heart, Miss Macayla. I know what your brother's dealing with, and if he's as resourceful as you, he'll be alright."

So desperately she wanted to believe him. With a nod, she swallowed against the rising fear that told her he must be wrong.

"I hope you're right." She stood, eager to leave.

How long before things would be right again? And Chase. She longed to forgive him. Had he always hid a temper or was this due to overwhelming circumstances, either from his injuries or years of service?

"You can go. Agent Averey will fill you in on anything else you might need to know."

Another nod.

"Thank you, again." With that, she slipped out.

Endless questions rolled through her head. Chase had another mission. While he did that, she'd do some research. She needed to understand him, otherwise, how would things ever work? If she didn't get a grasp on this, how could she help him? Guilt eroded her insides. If only she'd have dissuaded him from ever joining, then he wouldn't be dealing with whatever plagued him.

Chapter Fourteen

Chase

Chase struggled to focus on the details of his next plan. Thomas Knight Park, the location of his next assignment. He ran his hands over his head as Cassidy walked toward his car. His mind was going crazy. Control meant safety, sanity, peace of mind, and when it came to her, there seemed to be no such thing. Hearing what happened after he left nearly drove him to the brink of no return. In his absence the enemy struck, and he couldn't protect her.

Maybe if he could further control her actions, movements, maybe then she'd be safe. How had he allowed himself to slack so badly? Once they arrived at the next place he'd keep a tighter grip on the situation, on her, or die trying. Anything less would only mean failure. His memory went back to the safe-house.

"Didn't I warn you before about being careful with your phone?" He pressed as she shut the passenger side door.

Staring agape, she sat, frozen in uncertainty for a moment before answering.

"I didn't know that was going to happen, and I haven't been using my phone. You of all people should know I have nobody to talk to right now!"

He shook his head.

"You need to use your head! Awareness is of the utmost importance! You don't use your head and that leaves too many loose ends for the enemy to work with. Where's your phone now?"

She buckled her seatbelt, clearly shaken.

"I left it in the trash can at the motel. Mercer told me to upload what was on it to your laptop, wipe the memory, and destroy it, so that's what I did. Smashed it to bits."

A sigh of relief escaped him.

"Good. From now on, we are going to do things a little differently. You're going to do what I say, how I say, when I say. Is that understood?"

She looked confused, afraid.

"Wh-why do you want to control me? I don't understand. I didn't make him find me. It's not like I waved a big giant flag that said 'here I am, come get me'. What did I do that was so wrong? Some women might not like that. A lot would assume you're trying to manipulate them or something."

He gritted his teeth. She didn't understand. Control meant the difference between chaos and order, things being done right - the first time, between success and failure, and especially life and death for him and those around him. In circumstances like this, it meant everything.

"I need to take control of this situation, of you, your actions. Whatever your opinion is of control, and of me trying to control you, it's irrelevant. You need start considering every angle because they are. If you want to see your brother again, you can't afford anymore reckless mistakes. As far as your car is concerned, when they're done working on it, you don't get it until you change the plates. Got it?"

"I'm not a soldier or an agent, Chase! This is your world, not mine. How can you expect me to just get it? And if I don't understand something right away, are you going to get mad and go off on me like you did in the motel? I want to understand you, but sometimes it's hard, and patience is a virtue. If you expect me to learn something, you need to have the patience to help me, for me figure it out."

"It's simple, Cassidy. Simply do what I say, and we'll be fine. I know what I'm doing, and I've almost never lost a soldier or agent who's followed my orders to a T. I realize you're not a soldier, but perhaps you need to start thinking like one."

Her brows scrunched in a lost expression.

"How am I supposed to do that?"

Chase started the car.

"You'll learn what you need to from me."

With a gulp she tilted in acknowledgment.

"OK."

He made way, on to the next motel. Unable to help himself, he glanced over.

"What are your views on control? You seem to speak against it, yet, you act the submissive."

She squirmed a moment.

"Well, I guess I'm someone who's selectively submissive. Besides what I've dealt with in my childhood, I've had people try to manipulate me before, use me for their own purpose, and take off. It's not that I'm opposed to all authority, I just don't want to be someone's doormat. Someone you just bark orders at, and my thoughts, ideas, and opinions don't matter. They should matter!" She ran her fingers through silken honey tresses.

"To be in control is to be dominant, in authority. To be in authority is to be in a position to lead. You want to control me? You're my boyfriend, so let's say I accepted that. Will you take my suggestions and ideas into consideration, or will you merely dismiss me altogether when I see things differently, then tell me what I think is irrelevant, again? A good leader listens to the issues of those he leads before making his final decision, accepts he doesn't know everything, and if he hears a suggestion that might be useful with his, or better than his, he'll seriously consider using it."

He opened his mouth to speak, but she raised a hand to silence him. His eyes widened. Never before had she rebutted him that way.

"I get a little more of the concept of control than you realize, about the dynamics of dominance and submission. I have no problem being submissive to someone's authority as long as they're not trying to railroad me and treat me like crap. Been there, done that. I'm not going to submit to someone if I'm nothing more than a pawn. If you can accept me as having valuable ideas to contribute, and won't deal harshly with me, then fine. You must realize after what you said to me in the motel, and now, by telling me what I think is irrelevant, I have reason to question your motives."

He blinked. Once again, she proved to be an enigma, and he'd been less than kind.

"Am I clear?"

Was it wrong to picture her clad in a leather cat suit with a whip?

"You're right, I'm sorry. I shouldn't have said that."

Unvoiced questions appeared in her eyes. No question she worried about him. Could she understand the toll that his work had taken on his life? He'd dealt with much since joining, and between his head injury resulting in amnesia, and this last incident with the enemy getting the drop on them, he felt close to the edge of sanity.

She offered a faint smile.

"We'll figure this out together. As long as you don't give up, I won't either."

He nodded.

Nearly a half hour of silence passed before they arrived at the motel in South Portland. Another run-down shit-hole surrounded by trees, a short drive from South Portland Gardens. Uncertainty wafted from her. Had he taken another step toward losing her?

After helping him bring in their things she sat on the queen sized bed, appearing winded. The room was a step up from the last one. Similar lay out but everything was newer, including the wall mounted television, and navy blue carpeting on the floor. A complete contradiction of the exterior. It even had a fresh, clean smell, unlike the slight stale odor of the previous motel. The bathroom also seemed an upgrade. Blue tile flooring and matching blue tub and marble counter-top. Cassidy held her stomach.

"You alright?"

She smiled and swallowed.

"Fine, just a bit queasy, that's all."

Surely she needed a doctor, but he didn't dare take her anywhere public until the danger for her had passed. He tried not to think about it, desperate to hold on to whatever remaining sanity he possessed. For the first time, he felt in way over his head.

"Hungry? I'll run out and get you something to eat. I'll still get you that tea and whatever else, but you are not leaving this motel, got it?"

She seemed hesitant to speak. He approached, placing his hands comfortingly on her biceps.

"I won't be long, and nobody knows you're here. There's no way for anyone to track you here. You're safe, as long as you don't leave. OK?"

"Yeah. OK."

The delicate vulnerability she exuded tore through his chest, similar to when she'd witnessed his first seizure. He leaned in, brushing his lips against hers in a reassuring kiss.

"I won't let anything happen to you. Promise."

He caressed her cheek. She nodded, shaking slightly. Perhaps the whole incident and the potential outcome had sunk in, or perhaps it was something else.

"OK."

As he rushed around trying to get anything he thought she'd want and need, he considered his next move. The next location requiring his attention was ideal. The distance between the parking lot and his vantage point was short, and he'd have their meeting table beneath the bridge bugged before they even arrived. He'd finally be able to track Tony to his headquarters, and hopefully Cassidy's brother.

The sense of lacking control over this situation would be over soon, but once this mission was complete, what would he do? Leaving for months or a year on a normal basis is hard enough on a relationship, but the idea of leaving her while pregnant killed him. He'd miss out on ultrasound appointments to see his unborn child, being there for her at her most vulnerable.

What if something happened? What if while called away she miscarried, or had the child prematurely? A multitude of potential problems flashed in his brain. It wasn't definite yet, depended on what they found out, how things went down with Tony, but the possibility remained that Mercer would send him to Saudi Arabia for another intelligence mission.

That was just one of the things they were discussing when Cassidy called. Hearing gunshots over the phone from his seat left him paralyzed with fear until Mercer started talking to her once more. It was then that something snapped in his head. He would never allow that to happen again.

Retirement had never been something he'd considered, but he didn't want her to have to deal with things by herself. Even if she was a strong enough woman to handle it alone, she shouldn't have to. He wanted to be the kind of man who wasn't absent in his child's life, longed to be a positive influence. How could he do that if he had to travel thousands of miles away for months or a year at a time?

He was still reflecting on these things when he returned with two arm loads of parcels. The final question looming in his mind was - how would she take it if– or when–he told her he had to go?

"I brought you a chicken salad, the ginger tea you asked for, and some other stuff that might help."

She appeared from the bathroom, wiping her mouth with the back of a hand, other one on her stomach. Knots twisted in his gut. He was impatient for this to stop. It was agonizing watching her suffer.

"Thanks." Her voice cracked slightly as she sat on the bed.

He handed her the salad. It didn't seem safe to leave her alone for any length of time. Was he simply being overprotective? In this case, was that even possible? They sat on the bed, and he pulled out a steak sub while she started on her salad.

"I hate to leave you alone again, but I have to go out scouting tonight." Her eyes widened, near panic. "It's OK, just a few hours."

She stared down at her salad, toying with the fork.

"How do you always learn where they'll be?"

"Someone on the inside."

"You mean a spy?"

He eyed her silently. Her worry was apparent.

"How often does it go wrong?" Where was this coming from?

"Don't worry about those things, worry about yourself right now. You have someone in there to consider, so you need to eat."

She stabbed a few leaves and put them in her mouth. After swallowing she peered at him.

"Remember when we used to spar together?"

He swallowed the bite of his sub.

"Yeah?"

"I realize I can't do that right now, but perhaps we could find another way to workout together? Do videos or something?"

"I've got a lot going on right now, I'd have to think about it. Just too much on my mind to worry about that."

With a pout she returned to the meal before her.

"Oh, OK. Well, if you change your mind, let me know."

Why did she find that answer so displeasing? Was she even in any condition to do that? What made the thought even cross her mind? Tempting as it was to see her skin glistening with sweat once again, with so much going on, so much stress to deal with, he had to focus on the mission, and avoid thinking about anything else.

He suspected he'd done enough already and feared she was losing trust in him. It was possible the concussion that caused his amnesia left more damage than he thought and left him more insecure than usual.

"OK."

Cassidy moved closer, careful not to spill her salad.

"Promise you'll be careful."

He planted a gentle kiss to her temple.

"Always am."

As she leaned against him he sensed her fatigue. Once finished with her food, she lay her head in his lap, and conked out. Not much time had passed since he found out about her pregnancy and already he was grateful for not being a woman. All the stress on top of that likely didn't help.

The first measure of peace and quiet they had in a while and he didn't want to ruin it. Going over the names and info in the file Mercer handed to him again gave him nothing new. In his last meeting with the Sergeant Major he learned they were so close to something. They'd gotten into the emails which contained mountains of evidence for Tony and Aiden's activities. Instinct told him it was only a matter of time before he got a date for deployment.

When Cassidy woke from her nap, she laid into the punching bag he'd propped against the wall while she slept, but after a half hour was too winded to continue. Even then, she waited a couple of minutes before trying again. Another ten minutes and she gave up.

He straightened in the chair, turning his focus away from the laptop screen to her.

"Should you be pushing yourself so hard?"

"I'm fine." She managed between huffs as she plopped on the end of the bed to catch her breath.

"Cassidy..."

"I said I'm fine!"

He didn't dare push even though every protective instinct flew into overdrive. Last thing he needed was to cause more damage between them. Besides, she'd been through enough already.

"Anything I can do?"

"No, I just need to catch my breath." She shook her head.

Sweat drenched her clothing, causing her blue shirt to cling to her body like a second skin. Her hair matted to her face, the overall vision heated his blood, but his protective nature won out. Funny how he could face down a horde of enemy combatants without blinking, but one pregnant female and he was all twisted up inside, as nervous and confused as a lost puppy.

"Alright."

As she showered he prepped for his evening excursion. Temptation taunted him to go in with her, but reason kept him at bay. Instead he threw himself into preparation. This one would be different, the end was close, he could feel it.

"Getting ready to leave?" Seeing her come out wrapped in just a towel nearly killed his self-control.

"Yeah, I only have a couple of hours before I go."

She leaned against the post at the entrance of the bathroom.

"I don't suppose you're up for anything right now?"

There's was no mistaking the invitation in her eyes, and his body fired up in affirmation, but after seeing how she was before the shower, he feared it might be too much for her. He offered an appreciative smile.

"As tempting as that is, I think you need to slow down." A laugh of uncertainty escaped her lips.

"I'm not made of glass, I won't break."

"No, of course not, but you're worn out from your workout, and who knows what overexertion can do to you or the baby. I'm just trying to be careful, that's all."

"Oh, OK." A frown formed on her face as she sauntered to her bag, grabbed some clothes, and dressed.

"I didn't mean to offend you."

"It's fine."

She flopped in the bed and clicked on the television. He heaved an exasperated sigh as he finished up.

"Why don't we watch something together?"

"What do you have in mind?" She asked as he crawled in beside her, wrapped an arm around her.

"Seinfeld?" A smile, good start.

"Sure."

Time flew by and before he knew it, it was time to go. After what happened last time he left her alone, he couldn't help the apprehension taking over. He knew it was absurd, and eagerness to finish the whole ordeal overcame him.

"I'll be back as soon as I can. Until then, just relax, OK?"

"Yeah, OK."

As he left, he fought his rising insecurities. Things would go right, they had to.

Chapter Fifteen

Cassidy

As soon as Chase walked out the door, she went to his laptop and started her search. PTSD, a prominent result in her search, was worse than she imagined. Her heart broke. Might it explain why he reacted the way he did toward her, his stubborn insistence on misreading her, and his tenacious hold on wanting to always be right? She ran a hand through her hair. Somehow, she must have triggered it, when he started feeling out of control, because of her, he got irritated, and saw her as his enemy.

Might it also explained why he so desperately hated the idea of losing control of his environment and those around him, why he so easily roused to anger over finding out about the pregnancy? Was he having night terrors? If she asked, would he acknowledge it? There remained no doubt he hid things from her. Maybe he could hide some things from her, but not everything.

It killed her that he so quickly jumped the gun and misinterpreted the situation so badly, so wrong. Rather than listen, he immediately thought the worst of her. She shuddered.

He couldn't keep going like this, dynamite ready to blow. When would it happen again? What if she couldn't carry to term and miscarried, would he blame her? Tears flooded her cheeks. What could she do? If he was so worried about her why didn't he just retire?

She continued searching, trying to figure out any way to help him. Remembering their conversation on the phone years ago when he told her he wanted to join the army, she was culpable for everything. Why would he have called her if not for help to make his decision? Like a fool she assumed he'd already made up his mind.

Though given the chance to dissuade him, she should have, but didn't. Instead, in trying to be supportive, she'd inadvertently caused this, at least in part, his pain and misery. Whatever demons he dealt with were in part because of her. A sob escaped. It was no different to her than if she'd gone and given his enemy a weapon and issued the order to fire. All his harsh words, she deserved it, all of it. If things didn't work between them, she alone bore full responsibility.

You reap what you sow, Cassidy...

She wanted to help him somehow, at least ease his suffering. Perhaps her mistakes weren't capable of being erased, but she loved him, would do whatever possible to help. It wasn't much, but it was something.

Some of the solutions were not what she expected. Video games for example. It made little sense to her why playing something that recreated a battle in any way would help, but several sources cited it helped for coping with traumatic experiences, among other things, so she wouldn't knock it. Also, comedies, exercise, meditation, tai chi, counseling, anti-anxiety medication, anti-depressants, medicinal marijuana, and some questionable, potentially addictive pain medication.

Then there was something called Tapping, Acupoint Stimulation, Emotional Freedom Technique, so many names for the same thing. It confused her how tapping on different parts of the body reduced stress and anxiety, but with so many sources swearing by it, it had to be useful.

She gulped hard, drowning in the overwhelming sense of helplessness. He was not a stupid man, held a great deal of pride, and hated the idea of needing help, at least from her experience assisting him when he dealt with amnesia. If he perceived the idea of needing help as a weakness, and realized what she was doing, would he be grateful, or hate her forever? If he misread her again and decided to go full scorched-earth on her, her heart wouldn't survive the fallout.

She ran her fingers once more through soft strands in frustration while looking at the screen. Some of these things were impossible for her to provide and trying to persuade him to seek professional help and take medication would only lead to a massive argument. Exercise, comedies, video games, tai chi and meditation seemed most plausible. Would mentioning tapping be useful, or should she start out more subtle than that? Of all those, exercise appeared the best place to start, even though her earlier suggestion got shot down, likely also the comedy thing. It wouldn't be easy, but something needed done.

She thought about their conversation in the car. Her brain scrambled to understand. No one had ever flat out told her they wanted to control her, or her actions before. At that moment, she realized her brain wasn't only broken, but fragmented into a trillion pieces, scattered to the wind never to be found again, and there remained no help for her.

Despite what happened in the last motel, with his harsh insults, what he said in the car had reached a dark side of her. One where she knelt, nipping a nail on one hand in wicked anticipation, gently twisting a few strands of hair around a finger on the other, saying 'Woah baby, please go easy on me!'.

It stirred her insides with enough heat to melt his tires off their rims. It left her wanting to push his buttons to entice him to exert it more. If he were emperor or king a couple thousand years ago, she'd almost bet he'd have had one hell of a harem. Just thinking of how he might do so left her imagination once again running away from her, to that dark place that had her missing her pocket rocket. Clearly, her mind was nearly as twisted as Harley Quinn's.

That was dangerous and left her mentally scratching her head. If anyone else said that to her, she'd have sent them running. Coming from him, it was a potent linguistic aphrodisiac. The man did not play fair at all, and she probably needed therapy worse than anyone. After he said that, her brain had rushed to self-preservation mode, while her body still reeled from his admission. It took a while for her brain to register fully the words that followed.

After all, she didn't really know where they stood. She was uncertain whether he would go off again, and while she wanted to give him a chance, help him, she feared the worst. Instinct told her that once again, she'd end up alone. One of several reasons she refused to allow him to see he had so much influence over her, why she needed time to rebuild trust in him, that he wouldn't break her heart again.

What she'd read, also instilled more incentive to be careful. She didn't want to upset him. An impossible balance to strive for. This would take time to process.

Unsure what else to do to kill time, and rather than think about how much like a caged animal she felt, she hurriedly checked her email, Facebook, then returned to Chase's punching bag, laying into it a second round as if that would solve all her problems. Keeping fit was supremely important now, and if Chase knew what little control he had over this situation, there was no telling what he'd do, other than blame her.

Every so often she paused to give her right arm a shake. Chase had done a number on it. The redness had gone, but any jerk or pressure on her arm sent a jolting pain to that spot. She'd done everything to mask it while he was there. A brief examination showed no swelling or broken bones. Was that normal? From the look on his face, he was just as surprised as she that his goal hadn't succeeded. Also, he hadn't meant to hurt her.

She continued through the pain for nearly an hour before exhaustion won out. After another cool shower, she collapsed in the bed. Sleep had nearly claimed her when the sound of a notification coming from the laptop startled her.

With effort she rose and checked. Breathing became difficult. Nausea bubbled in her stomach as she stared at the photo of a bloody severed finger on the screen. To breath became impossible. She wanted to scream.

It had to be Tony, or one of his men. Who else would do such a monstrous thing? Hacking Stacy's account was bad enough. Obviously the sender knew the account holder was dead and tied to her since they probably saw Stacy's obituary in the paper. Another message.

Do I have your attention now? Be at Knightville Landing in one hour. No more delays. Don't tell anyone what you're doing, no help. If you try to pull one over on me, the next thing to go will be his head.

After threatening to remove his fingers if she didn't comply, they did. She clutched her throat. There remained no doubt in her mind they weren't bluffing about this either. Her poor brother! If he remained alive until Chase managed to mount a rescue, it would be a miracle, but that could take days, if not weeks. Joe didn't even have an hour.

Heart racing, she stood, paced frantically. She knew she shouldn't reply, but her brain was far from functional at the moment.

How can I be sure my brother's still alive? Let me see him!

The reply came immediately.

Be there, or he won't be...

Time ran out. She rushed to get ready. With any luck she would find a way to save him, Sheila, and get them all out alive. Armed to the teeth, she flew out the door and to the lobby, had the employee call a taxi, and waited. In minutes one had arrived, and she was on her way. It would take some time to get there, hopefully she wouldn't be too late.

Chapter Sixteen

Chase

Wind rustled the bushes as he crouched, watching for Tony's vehicle. With more than enough time to set up, he eagerly awaited the chance to place the tracking device on Tony's SUV. This time, he would get the upper hand.

Ever since the blowout at the motel, even though Cassidy had given him another chance, he sensed a shift. Their argument in the car only made things worse. No question, he'd shaken her trust, and he sensed darkness looming ahead.

From her body language, her reactions to him, it couldn't be more obvious she liked a man who exuded power, or at least when he did. She outright lied, and that stung deep. He recognized a defense mechanism when he saw one, when that wall came up. She feared him. He was losing her. Perhaps turning her down earlier had hurt things. It sliced through his heart like a knife. He fought to shake away the thoughts, forcing himself to concentrate on the task at hand.

Black clouds rolled in as the air cooled and the sky darkened. Tires on pave graced his ears before the beams from Tony's headlights flashed across the lot. Moments later, other vehicles followed, parked. Several men proceeded down the nearby wooden ramp, dressed in hooded black shirts, far behind Tony.

"This had better be good." One man gritted his teeth. "I don't get it, why all this trouble for some dumb broad? No way she'd know anything on that laptop. It makes no sense why they'd tell her, and Agent Averey won't willingly follow her into a trap."

"I heard she's actually an agent for Homeland Security or the FBI or some shit. Think about it! How else would she have escaped, gotten away with our info? She still communicates with the Sergeant Major, captured that stupid rat we released from his cage, and knows Agent Averey's location. No average bitch could slip away that many times. Imagine what information we'll get from her."

The taller of the group shook his head. Another snickered.

"Say what you want, it's just dumb luck. We're just here to rig the bridge, then when the time comes... boom."

"You don't think she's actually going to show, do you, even after the message we sent her?"

"She will, she knows what'll happen if she doesn't."

As their voices drifted away, Chase crept to Tony's SUV and attached the small device to the frame, trying not to think about what they implied. Once in place, he made way to his equipment. It took everything to focus while teetering on the brink of madness. Never before had a woman messed up his head so badly, left him grasping for sanity. In the field that kind of distraction usually meant disaster.

He barely heard them as his mind wandered, refusing to stay away from Cassidy. She was going to run away again, he could feel it, and his mind, heart wouldn't be able to handle that again. The pain of that knowledge seared him, the idea that this was one battle he couldn't win. As he ran a hand over his head, the approaching sound of footsteps stole his attention.

Their meeting had concluded, Tony was leaving. He waited until every last man had gone before contacting Mercer while ensuring the blip showed up on his screen. It was moving. Good.

"Good to go."

"Excellent. Follow him. Once the location has a fix, contact me. I'll send in a team, we'll strike tonight."

"Yes, Sir."

With every ounce of will he kept his sight focused on his target, reigning in his thoughts. If she hurt him this time, she'd feel the full fury of his pain. Suffer like an enemy on the battlefield, then be out of his life for good.

Nearly an hour had passed before his target stopped. Crawling at snail pace he watched as Tony exited his vehicle and entered the massive, isolated brick building nestled at the end of a dirt road, surrounded by trees. Darkness had fallen, serving as camouflage for his vehicle as he parked a fair distance away.

The sky broke open as thunder rumbled and lightning flashed across the sky. He called Mercer again and gave the location.

"Scout the perimeter, then contact me with your info."

"Yes, Sir."

He grabbed some equipment, ammo, and weapons from the trunk, prepped them, then skulked toward the building, using the trees for cover, pulling the hood over his head. Any information he could provide about the area was vital. There'd only be one shot at this.

Cameras sparsely dotted the building, large windows were blacked out, a metal door in the back was electronically locked. Two cameras hung above both front and back doors, complete with sensor lights. There had to be a way to shut down the power to the building, and knock out the visuals, or hack their system.

Scanning overhead, blinking against the rain, he detected a wire which led to a power grid on the corner of the building, in a small blind spot from the cameras. He hoped they didn't have a backup generator.

A thorough examination of the surrounding area showed the darkness and forest would provide excellent cover for an undetected approach up to about twenty meters from the construct. He retrieved the Eagle 5P from his bag, switched it on, then aimed at the building.

A real beehive of activity carried on within, the most occurring on the second of the three floors, which had a call center atmosphere with a cafeteria. The first housed what appeared to be some conference and meeting rooms as well as several offices, sparsely populated. The top looked like some kind of dormitory, mostly empty, with possibly four bathrooms.

Half of the basement served as storage for weapons, miscellaneous items, and unknown substances. The other half, set apart by bars, held two people who sat on the floor, male and female, apparently communicating. The male seemed to be missing a finger. His jaw tensed. If that was Cassidy's brother, she was going to be furious.

Between the armed men stalking each floor, the workers hustling among the storage, and those guarding the caged off area, he counted no less than thirty heavily armed men. At least there was no sign of a generator.

He retreated to the blackened cover of the trees, formulated a plan, and called the Sergeant Major.

"We need someone to infiltrate security and visuals, set up a replay loop for the cameras, and a team to infiltrate the premises. This is a rescue mission for two captives, take no prisoners. When I find Tony, I'll deal with him myself."

"If possible, I want Tony alive. We need to interrogate him."

He wanted to kill the bastard, but an order was an order.

"Understood."

Nearly an hour passed waiting by his vehicle until backup arrived in a couple of black armored vehicles. A team in full black body armor, armed to the teeth. A woman approached from behind the vehicles, a no-nonsense expression on her face, dark hair held up in a bun, sienna eyes focused. The rest stood behind, awaiting orders.

"What's the skinny?"

"You the hacker?"

She nodded sharply.

"Name?"

"Carson, Sir."

"Agent Carson, you need to circumvent their security, loop visuals from the cameras, and unlock the back door." Another nod of acknowledgement.

He peered behind her.

"Once she's in, move quickly, and with stealth. There are three floors and the basement. This is both a rescue, and intelligence operation. We are here to recover two captives, possible contraband in the basement, and retrieve all potential information from their computers and network." He scanned each man in the eye.

"You..." He pointed to a few men to his left. "Go to the basement, retrieve the captives, secure the contraband, take no prisoners."

His attention turned to those in the middle.

"Hit the second floor, secure all information, again, take no prisoners."

He focused on those remaining.

"Three of you will come with me on the first floor, the rest will secure the perimeter. Anything moves, shoot to kill."

"Yes, Sir!"

Agent Carson returned to the large cargo van parked behind the armored vehicles as everyone went into position, guns drawn. Chase accepted some body armor, put it on, then crouched by the back door, waiting. Seconds ticked by before his ears picked up the faint sound of a click. He slipped the door open and signaled to move.

Flanked by his small entourage, he hit each room, one by one, taking out everything in his path, using the chaos of the moment to his advantage. It wasn't until nearing the end of the hall that he reached Tony's office, and found him leaning back in his office chair, head resting against his palms, staring smugly.

"So, you found me. You must be proud of yourself." Tony leaned forward, bringing his arms to the desk, intertwining his fingers.

Ignoring the apparent mind games he nudged his jaw toward him.

"Take him into custody." Tony stood, smirking, as they approached.

He took a step back, a hand up to halt their approach.

"You have me now, but it's only a matter of time before we have what we need on you and your superiors."

"No time for games. Take this piece of shit and let's go."

A croaking laugh grated his ears as the phone on Tony's desk rang and he saw the number on the display.

"Just let me get this." He grinned and press the button for the speaker phone before anyone could take another step.

"Tony here."

"Cassidy just arrived."

Tony's eyes flashed, lips curled in a maniacal grin, a similar expression he'd seen on his brother's face before. Chase froze, jaw tensed to the point his teeth ground hard.

"Better late than never I suppose. There's been a change of plans. I'm a bit tied up at the moment, so just go straight to the second phase of the plan."

"Tony?" Confusion lined the man's voice.

"Extract and terminate! Are you really so incompetent that I have to repeat myself?"

"No, consider it done!"

Tony disconnected the call with a smirk.

"Better hurry agent, you don't have a lot of time. I'd wager about twenty minutes."

It took longer than that to get to Tony's headquarters. He fumed. She'd blatantly defied him. Why would she leave the motel? Was it him? Tony's doing? His blood boiled at her reckless, thoughtless actions. He'd have to teach her a lesson later.

"Take him and let's go. I'll deal with our newfound problem. Make sure you bind his ankles too, he does *not* get away." Chase ground out.

They quickly followed his instruction as he stormed out, punching the wall on the way. As he left the building agent Carson rushed to him.

"The mission was a success. I've informed our superior about the new development. He's sending in a team to help her." He waved her off.

"I got this." He turned to see most of his team regroup, the liberated male and female in their midst, wrapped in blankets and led to the cargo van where a pair of medics waited.

Their mistreatment was obvious. If Cassidy hadn't pulled such a foolhardy stunt, he might have given a shit. He thought he had this situation under control, he was wrong. Once again, she insisted on complicating everything.

"Chain Tony down with everything you've got, he doesn't go anywhere but point B. I even want him gagged. Where's the Intel?"

"We still have men inside working, but all threats have been neutralized." One man spoke matter-of-factly.

"Good. When you're done, hold it for me until I get back." He watched as two men chained Tony to a bench in the back of one of the armored vehicles. "I'm going to deal with a new problem."

He made haste toward his vehicle. There'd be hell to pay.

Chapter Seventeen

Cassidy

The downpour hadn't let up, and she wished she had a raincoat. Shivering against the chill creeping in she took in her surroundings before making her presence known. Even though they said no help, she didn't trust them to keep their word entirely, so she borrowed the taxi driver's cell and called Mercer, informing him of the situation.

After getting an earful from the Sergeant Major, he assured her help was on the way. While he made it clear she'd made a bad decision, at least he hadn't insulted and berated her, which brought on more questions about Chase and his behavior. She shook away the thoughts.

There were more important things to worry about, like how it looked like someone was rigging the support pillars of the bridge with something suspicious. The chill in her veins turned to ice as it dawned on her. They wanted to blow up the bridge, and her along with it!

The men had finally decided to stop gawking and approach. Every instinct told her to bolt.

"Cassidy?"

Her hand hovered over her firearm as she stepped back.

"Who's asking?"

The statuesque man retrieved a box from his jacket pocket, opened it. She retreated another couple of steps. Her brother's finger!

"Where is he? I don't cooperate unless I see him!"

Surrounded by water on the platform she could jump in, use the boats and surrounding darkness as cover if necessary. In one quick movement she had her gun trained on the closest of the three men. They too withdrew theirs.

"Don't be stupid, if you want him alive you'll come with us." Nausea bubbled up.

Not now...

She swallowed hard.

"I'm not going anywhere with you! I don't trust you. For all I know, he could already be dead and you're trying to lure me into a trap."

The men faced each other.

"You sure she's not an agent?" One man asked.

What gave them that idea?

"We're going for a little walk, you're going to tell us what we want to know."

She shook her head.

"What's there to tell? Your boss already knows Chase is alive. There's nothing left."

They laughed.

"You are in constant communication with Sergeant Major Mercer, contain knowledge about Agent Averey's ties to other branches of Homeland Security, and are privy to the information they possess, including possible mission details. We need that information."

She shook her head in bewilderment. They've surely lost their minds.

"I don't know anything, and I'm not an agent. You clearly need to reconsider your sources. Now release my brother and friend, we're done here."

They cocked their weapons.

"No, we're not." She fought against them but a hard knock to the head sent her to the ground.

When her eyes opened again, she was staring at the underside of the bridge. Thunder and lightning crashed above before the roar of several armed men rushed forward, covered head to toe in black body armor, brandishing automatic weapons. Gunfire erupted as she rubbed the bump on her head.

It was impossible to shake the ringing in her ears or the throbbing pain from her head. This was not going well at all. A familiar pair of steely arms hoisted her up, holding her against a muscular chest. With great effort she peered into Chase's angry eyes.

"Chase, I..."

He glared daggers.

"Don't, Cassidy, just... Don't." Too weak to try again, she collapsed against him.

When her lids fluttered open once more she found herself back in the motel room, dry, wearing different clothes. It was still night and she could hear the sound of the rain and wind blowing outside. The pain from earlier had ebbed away, replaced by a fresh wave of nausea. Turning her head she noticed Chase on his laptop, examining the picture in her messenger.

"You should have listened to me, should have stayed here." He turned to her, blue eyes blazing.

"They cut off his finger, Chase! What, I'm supposed to just let them kill him?"

"It was a trap. They were going to blow up the bridge, and you along with it, after they got whatever info they assume you have. Your brother wasn't even there."

She sat up, frustration pouring from her lips.

"Oh? I suppose you've figured out where he is? Hmm? All this time nobody found him, and they started chopping off his digits like they said they would. They said if I didn't show, they'd kill him. And I'm not supposed to take that seriously?"

"We found them. Your brother. Sheila. They're in the hospital right now. But if you'd used your fucking head and listened to me, instead of putting yourself and our unborn at risk..." Chase stood, a roar of anguish escaped him.

"Do you ever consider the consequences before you act? What have I told you about awareness? You should never trust the enemy! But you didn't think, and if I hadn't arrived with backup, you'd be dead right now! You're a fucking idiot!"

That hit, hard. Her heart shredded. She threw her arms in the air in defeat.

"That's unfair! I'm not a soldier or an agent, and it's wrong of you to expect me to think like one. And it doesn't make me an idiot simply because I don't think the same way you do, or don't understand everything you try to tell me! I try to see your point of view, but sometimes it's hard! I've never been on a battlefield overseas, or had to do intelligence missions, all I can do is try to put myself in your shoes and empathize, but it'll never be enough for you!"

His eyes widened, a wide array of emotions played across them.

"You're just being insecure. Don't worry so much."

She sucked in a breath. Was he kidding?

"What the hell? You told me that my opinion and perception don't matter to you. That tells me *I* don't matter to you. Now you have the nerve to tell me I'm just being insecure? That's so cold!"

She stood abruptly, swaying momentarily as a wave of dizziness swept over her. Chase rose quickly, rushing to side.

"Cassidy, what are you doing?"

"I want you to take me to the hospital. I need to see my brother."

He shook his head.

"No, you need your rest. I can take you tomorrow."

"Chase!"

"Tomorrow..." Her eyes narrowed but he wouldn't budge.

"Fine." She grumbled in frustration, heading for the door.

"Where are you going?"

"For a walk."

"In that? You're pregnant! You'll get sick! Are you insane?" She scoffed.

"I'm not sugar, I won't melt. Excuse me."

She threw on her sneakers and strapped on her weapons.

"Have you lost your mind? I'll take you for a drive, I'll walk with you, but you're not going out there by yourself!"

"Why?" She glared. "Is Tony out there now? Is he going to get me?"

"No, but..."

"Then let me be, I want to be alone, and since you don't want me getting my car 'til my plates get changed..." Ignoring his shocked expression she stormed out the door, slamming it behind her.

By the time Chase had the mind to follow she'd already made it to the sidewalk and out of view, but she could still faintly hear the curses proceeding from his mouth.

How had things between them gotten so bad? He seemed so inclined to blame her. Was it her fault? Tears blended with rain down her cheeks. This was killing her. Was there no end to his cruelty?

Chapter Eighteen

Chase

Why would she have done something so dangerous, so stupid? First she took off on a fools mission, and now this. He slammed the door as he stormed back into the motel. When he saw the handle of that gun crashing down on her head at the landing, he nearly lost it. Not wasting any time, he'd sent in everything he had.

He didn't care about her possible intentions. The road to hell is always paved with good intentions. Case in point. If he hadn't arrived just in time, she never would have made it out alive. He whipped the punching bad across the room in a roar of frustration. It slammed against the wall and fell to the floor with a loud thud.

It nearly killed him leaving her alone again while she slept, in case she woke up, but he had to retrieve the info the team had collected and speak with Mercer. Things had really started to go to south. In a last second decision, he strapped his sidearm on his belt, threw on his shoes and a raincoat from his bag, and took off after her.

It didn't matter what she said. It wasn't safe for her out alone in her condition. Especially at night. It didn't take long to track her down, he only needed to follow the fresh track of muddy shoe prints along the side of the road.

"Cassidy! Seriously! What the hell do you think you're doing?"

"Walking."

"In the rain, are you insane? Come back to the motel, we don't have to talk about what happened. Please, come back where I know you're safe!" She stopped abruptly, and he bumped against her.

"I'm pregnant, not a fragile weakling, stop treating me like one! I'm fully capable of taking care of myself!"

To say he felt out of his element would be an understatement at this point. Her stubborn streak truly rivaled his own.

"I'm well aware you can take care of yourself, that's not..."

"Then what?"

"It can be dangerous out this time of night. What if something happens while you're out by yourself? Who knows the extent of Tony's reach? What if you have a medical emergency or something?" She flung her arms up in the air.

"Oh my god! I'm just going for a walk! There hasn't been one car on this road since I left, and nobody knows where we're staying. You're being paranoid!"

Was he? He ran his hands over his head, sending massive drops of water flying.

"Lots of things can happen. I don't want anything to happen to you, please!"

She started off again, quickening her pace.

"I'll be fine, and right now, you're annoying me. Go. Away."

"No! Come on, don't be so foolish!"

"Leave me alone. I'll be back soon enough."

He tried to keep up, but she quickened her pace again. She hustled pretty fast for someone in her condition.

"Cassidy!"

Silence.

"CASSIDY!"

Eventually he gave up. She was hellfire when angry and this was going nowhere. It tore him up having to retreat, but this amounted to entering foreign territory blindfolded. His cell rang as he neared the door of the motel.

"Good work agent. We'll get to work on this first thing. I'll tell you tomorrow if your deployment is a go."

"Understood."

He ran his hands over his head. How would Cassidy react if he did get sent off? Calling her on that stupid stunt pissed her off, yet he hadn't been wrong. Might this be a hormonal issue, or something else? Usually she was far more reasonable than this. After twenty minutes he ran back out to find her. The rain had stopped, but she was still nowhere in sight. The woman had to be crazy! Then again, so was he for letting her go. He just wanted to forget this day.

After taking a few steps in the direction she went, the sound of nearby rustling reached his ears. Hand hovering over his weapon he followed the sound. After rounding the corner toward the back of the motel, frustrated mumbling became apparent. He couldn't help but grin. Perhaps she still maintained a sense of reason after all.

He hustled over to the side of his car where she sat, head leaning against the door.

"So this is where you're hiding."

She smiled sheepishly.

"Yeah..."

He sat, wrapping an arm around Cassidy's shoulders.

"It's getting late and I think we both had a rough day. Let's go back and watch something together. Relax. Call it a day. Things will look better tomorrow, and you'll get to see your brother, and Sheila."

She nodded, stifling a yawn.

"Alright."

Chapter Nineteen

Cassidy

Her eyes blinked against the bright light that filled the room. It was a new day, one in which she no longer needed to worry about Tony, his goons, or Steve, trying to hurt her. To top it all off, Joe and Sheila were finally free. She would go to the hospital to see them, pick up her car, then finally make an appointment with her doctor. It was about time.

She looked over at Chase's sleeping form. The last long while had been rocky, but now they could finally get past the stress, everything, and focus on making things better between them. She could try a few of the techniques designed to help him. Hopefully, he'd appreciate the effort.

Queasiness started up, and she sat. Peering over she noticed a box of saltines on the nightstand. How thoughtful. She smiled, reached over, and took out a few before putting them back.

As she nibbled on them she wondered if she should go pick up the car by taxi or wait for Chase to wake up. She wasn't long wondering before he awoke.

"Hey." The corner of his lips curled in a way that sent familiar flutters to her stomach.

"Morning." She replied.

Chase yawned, stretched, then sat up.

"Chase, can we please go to the hospital?" He laughed.

"Pushy, aren't we?"

"Come on, please! I want to see that they're OK!"

With a groan he arose and dressed.

"Alright, just let me make a phone call, then we'll go."

Upon arrival he led her to the room where they lay, their beds side by side, the curtain between them open. Despite having been cleaned up and cared for, they still looked like hell. Scrapes and bruises covered both of them. She rushed to give them each a gentle hug, trying not to disturb the tubes and needles. For whatever reason, Chase stayed out in the hall, sat in a chair, and waited.

"Oh my! I'm so glad you guys are OK!"

"We're fine now. We thought we'd never get out of there." Sheila exclaimed.

Cassidy turned to Joe, staring at his bandaged hand, tears forming.

"God, Joe!" She took his wrist, carefully bringing it up for closer examination. "I'm sorry I didn't get here sooner!"

He let out a low chuckle.

"It's OK. We were held for overnight observation in a different ward. You'd never have been allowed in."

"How did you manage your withdrawals?"

He patted her hand and smiled.

"Sheila. She managed to grab my bag of Oxy's and hide them while I caused a pretty good distraction. There were so many of them, and when they told us what they were planning, I knew we weren't getting away. Didn't stop me from trying though. A few of them required stitches, a couple of casts... You know me."

That was her brother, a scrapper with little to no fear. She shook her head with a grin.

"Yeah, I do."

After a few minutes Chase popped his head in the doorway, wriggling his finger in summon.

"Hold on a sec." She told Joe and approached him.

"I got a call, I need to leave right away. You alright here for a while?"

"Yeah." How she missed her phone, and her car.

"Alright. I'll see you a little later." With that he left.

She returned to the room.

"Who's that?" Sheila peeked out from her bed, but saw nobody, only the woman sitting at the nurses' station.

"My boyfriend, Chase."

Sheila smiled, sat upright.

"What's he like?"

Heat flooded her cheeks, and she knew they had to be red. There were some things she didn't want to say. The last while had been rough after all, and she felt sure what drove him to irritation was somewhat her fault. She wanted to steer the conversation elsewhere, for the time being.

Not only that, she wasn't ready to share the fact that she was pregnant. Too soon. The riskiest time for even a normal pregnancy was the first trimester. She just had to have a condition that made hers that much more hazardous.

"He's a sweetheart, even though he deals with a lot. Has a rough job. So what happened to you guys? How did you get out?"

"It was frightening. Honestly, I thought we would die in there. Especially after what they did to Joe." Probably better Chase dealt with those responsible than she, otherwise, she'd have likely done something regrettable. "Every so often they'd ask us questions about you, but nothing made sense. When we finally did get rescued, it was all such a blur. We hid under a table when everyone started shooting." Cassidy gave each of them another hug, heart swelling.

They'd been through so much.

' "I'm so glad you guys are alright! When do you get to leave?"

"We'll be here for another couple of days, but we'll have to go for some kind of psych evaluation. Something about trauma." Joe raised his wrapped hand with a frown. "They couldn't find the finger, but even if they had, it's been too long."

"Oh, Joe, I'm so sorry!" If she'd only have let them take her, none of this would have happened.

It was impossible not feel responsible.

"This isn't your fault, Cassy! Whatever they wanted, you're only a pawn stuck in the middle of something. You can't be blamed for that!"

The words did nothing to alleviate her guilt. Accepting that job a while back to help Chase had cost her so much, and still she suffered the repercussions. She bore some culpability, and while the enemies made their own choices to do what they did, her involvement was still a contributing factor. At least it was over now. Now, there remained the matter of acting as a witness if the courts should require it of her. Steve's last stunt went above and beyond, and she imagined it would require a higher court.

"Thanks, Joe."

He turned to Sheila.

"When we get out, the four of us should go on a double date." Sheila's eyes widened as she smiled.

"Sure."

Cassidy grinned. Nothing like a near death experience to bring out the bravado.

"Sounds like a great idea. I'll run it by him."

"Great."

The rest of the visit consisted of small talk. An hour ticked by, then two. Where was Chase?

Chapter Twenty

Chase

"Incredible!" Chase stared at the image of the compound on the monitor.

"Yes. Through what information we've gathered from emails and what we have so far from last night, there's reason to believe this is the location. This is where you need to go."

"When do I leave?" Mercer leaned back in his black office chair, folding his hands behind his head.

"Tomorrow."

Chase's eyes widened.

"That's sudden."

"As well as it went last night, Tony had enough time to warn someone about what happened. I don't believe it's a coincidence that the mole relaying info to and from Aiden mysteriously disappeared this morning either."

"Chase ran a hand over his head while gritting his teeth. *Just great...* Someone's gone ahead to warn them."

"Affirmative."

"Shit." This would not bode well with Cassidy, he was sure.

"We need to change our strategy. Our Intrusion Detection Specialist has detected a breach, focusing on our mission plans for Saudi Arabia, possibly in retaliation of last night. He's still trying to locate the source."

Chase nodded.

"There will be a private plane waiting for you at the back of the Bangor International Airport, equipped with our latest experimental ghost technology. I will meet you there for a last-minute briefing. It will take you and your team straight to Ryiadh Air Force Base in Saudi Arabia with the only stops being for refueling. We'll send your supplies and everything you need ahead of you. Be there for thirteen-hundred hours."

"Yes, Sir."

If Cassidy survived the time apart, he would owe her big time. He didn't want to be apart from her, especially given the pregnancy, but this was his livelihood. There was nothing he could do. His mind jogged back to a dinner conversation they had after she first witnessed him in a seizure.

Do you think you'll ever retire...?

He'd considered a few times since she asked. He loved his job, but he loved Cassidy. In his heart he knew he didn't want to leave her alone again.

"Any questions?"

"Yeah. How long will it take to process an application for retirement?"

The Sergeant Major seemed surprised.

"Even if you apply now, it might take a year. Are you sure you want to do this?"

"Yeah."

"Alright." After reaching into his bottom desk drawer, Mercer handed him a folder filled with papers.

A quick glance revealed several forms.

"This is a pre-retirement package. It will make things easier if you familiarize yourself with this and start gathering your info. We can get started upon your return, which will probably be in about six months. This will give you some time to think it over."

"Thank you, Sir."

"Any other questions?"

"Negative."

"Dismissed."

With a curt nod he left. He wanted to surprise Cassidy with his plan for retirement after returning from his mission. There was no doubt in his mind she'd be pleased. He knew she worried about it even if she didn't say anything.

At least the worst for her was over. Anyone who posed a threat to her had with. She could return to normal, whatever that may be after everything she'd lost. She had her brother, and a new friend, that surely counted for something.

The afternoon sun was exceedingly hot as he made way to his car, wasting no time turning on the air conditioning once inside. No matter how he told her about his sudden deployment, she was not going to be happy. He only hoped he could somehow soften the blow. Perhaps waiting until they returned to the motel would be best.

On the way to the hospital he decided a stop was mandatory. He hoped a nice surprise would help, but after their last two arguments realized she was the type of woman who either forgave you or didn't. No chocolates or flowers required. He only hoped this would be enough.

As he entered the large brick building, a curvaceous brunette in full dance getup approached him.

"Hello and welcome to Aquarius Ballroom Dance Studio. How may I help you today?" Her hazel eyes gave an appraising look.

"Is Jess in today?" He hoped so.

She was an old friend, a talented dancing instructor, and he knew Cassidy would feel comfortable with her.

"Just a second."

It wasn't long before the cute little redhead with blue eyes donning a shimmering blue dance outfit made her appearance.

"Hey Chase! I haven't seen you in a while. How have you been?"

"Doing great! I'm heading out tomorrow. I was just wondering if you had any spare time later to do a private lesson."

She stood thoughtful for a moment.

"I get out at eight. How many should I expect?"

"Two. Me, and my girlfriend."

"Excellent! Any idea what dance you want to practice?"

He considered his options.

"Not sure. Something easy."

"It would help if you told me a little about her. Does she like dancing?" Just the memory of watching her when they were holed up at Mercer's safe-house had him working to cool the heat threatening to ignite his libido.

"Yeah, she's pretty good."

She led him to a row of chairs in the nearby lobby and they sat.

"What experience does she have?"

"Pretty sure she's had belly dance lessons or something like it."

Her eyes lit up.

"Wonderful! So..." She clapped her hands together. "Let me guess. You're leaving for a tour of duty and you want to give her something to remember until you get back, and since you're coming to me last minute you only found on short notice. Am I correct?"

"Yeah."

"Since she's done belly dancing, she might be good at some of our Latin dances." He could see the wheels turning in her head. "I got it! How about Rumba? This would make for a smooth transition for her since she is already familiar with isolating hip movements and other similar movements that the Rumba requires."

Already his anxiety was bubbling up. Dancing wasn't his thing, but he'd try for Cassidy.

"Yeah, I'll try that."

"Perfect! You can stop by my place at nine. We'll practice in my basement studio. Do either of you have shoes?"

Shit!

"No."

"Don't worry, I'll find you guys some. She can go through mine. Just show up at my place at nine."

"Thanks."

She gave him a hug as they stood.

"Later." Jess exclaimed as he left.

Hopefully this would make the news of his leaving less of a hard pill to swallow. Cassidy certainly deserved something good. With any luck, for her sake, this would be his last mission.

Chapter Twenty-One

Cassidy

"Well, you two seem to be doing alright." The friendly blond doctor smiled at Sheila and Joe while she sat in a chair and listened.

"Here." The doctor said as she handed them each a card. "You'll be seeing doctor Steeves for your psych evaluation. She specializes in trauma cases, similar to yours."

"Great. Thanks Michelle!" Sheila reached up and hugged her warmly.

Michelle's eyes turned misty.

"Only the best for you. I'm so sorry about what you've been through!"

"Don't worry, I'm sure we'll be fine and she won't need to see us more than once."

The doctor nodded.

"I hope you're right. I'll see you later."

Not long after the doctor left, Chase knocked on the door frame.

"Time to go. I have a surprise for you. You don't have much time to get ready."

His eyes reflected mixed emotions, and she sensed he was hiding something other than whatever he had planned.

"OK." She turned to Joe and Sheila. "I guess I have to go. I'll talk to you guys later."

"Yep, later."

She followed in curious silence. It wasn't until after they sat in his car that he spoke.

"I'm being deployed to Saudi Arabia and I have to leave tomorrow afternoon."

Her lips parted in surprise. She knew this was part of his job but no matter when it happened, it would have been too soon. A part of her wanted to scream and cry, but that wouldn't solve anything. This was one of the things she'd always feared.

"There's something else. I've made arrangements with a dance instructor for tonight. We're taking a private rumba lesson."

Confusion festered. It left her so sad that he had to go, but it was so sweet that he'd try something based on a thing she enjoyed so much. Many men would reach for flowers and chocolates, he went for the things that mattered to her. Could all the negative behavior he previously expressed merely been stress?

"Oh, Chase!" She straddled his lap, pressing her lips to his in passionate appreciation.

He opened up to her with a groan as something hard pressed against her thigh, the heat burning through the fabric between them, sending fire into her veins. After a moment he reluctantly gave her a gentle nudge, a low rumble vibrating in his chest.

"We need to get ready. If you're still this grateful afterwards, we can certainly pick up where we left off." The way the corner of his lips curled up, along with the darkening of his eyes sent another wave of fire rushing the span of her body.

A blush crept in her cheeks.

"Right, sorry."

He stopped at the Maine Mall in South Portland.

"Let's get you something appropriate for the occasion." The heat from his hand as he placed it at the small of her back sent a shiver the length of her spine.

"You don't need to do that! I can buy it myself, but thank you anyway!"

He shook his head.

"I know, but I want to. I'll be gone for a long time and want you in something memorable."

"Oh..." Surely her whole body flushed.

After browsing a few stores he found a gorgeous metallic v-neck slip dress that reached her ankles and matching heeled sandals. It left her in stunned silence, feeling like an idiot. All that time she'd spent questioning him after his outbursts, and his attitude shifted the moment the danger had passed for them. She still intended to try some of the suggestions she'd read about when he came back, if he came back...

It was a struggle to push away the fear. He got injured last time he left, and it nearly killed him. However magical the evening, it wouldn't take away the inevitable months of anxiety that awaited.

They nearly reached the exit when he spoke.

"Everything OK, Cassidy? You're so quiet."

What could she say? *Please don't go, Chase! I love you! I don't want you to go!* Yeah, sounding like a desperate child wouldn't help at all. Nothing seemed to stop the frightening images of potential outcomes from flooding her head. Only this time, she couldn't run away from them. She knew this would eventually happen, yet when he asked her out, she still said yes.

"I'm fine. The dress is beautiful, thank you."

"You're welcome."

Even after stopping for a bite to eat and rushing to the motel to get cleaned up, dread consumed her, and nausea started again. Realizing that he'd miss out on ultrasounds and doctor visits, feeling the baby kick, assuming it went well, broke her heart all the more.

Come nine o'clock, he parked in a driveway before a beautiful two-story stone house. After giving her a slow scan of dark approval he opened the door.

"Let's go."

Standing nervously, she waited for the door to open after Chase rang the bell. A red haired woman wearing black yoga pants and matching tank top answered, bearing the appearance and figure of a professional dancer. Insecurity surfaced. She'd look like an idiot.

"Chase! Hi!" The woman greeted with a smile as she stepped back. "Please, come in."

Cassidy stepped in behind Chase as she led them to the basement.

"I'm glad to see you have shoes." She smiled. "I never got your name."

"It's Cassidy." As she spoke she extended her hand which the woman took.

"Jess. Pleasure to meet you." Jess turned to Chase. "There's a pair of shoes for you in the closet over there." She pointed across the expanse of polished hardwood flooring, to a door at the back of the room.

"Thank you, likewise."

"I understand you have some dance experience."

"A little. I've never done ballroom dancing before."

Jess cracked a grin.

"It's normal to be nervous. Don't worry, you'll do fine."

She hoped so. Last thing she wanted was to ruin the evening Chase worked for.

Chapter Twenty-Two

Chase

Cassidy looked amazing. Impatience to peel that dress off gnawed at him. Jess' clapping stole his attention. Low rhythmic music filled the air.

"OK, let's get started. We're going to begin with the box step. You two come together, put your arms out like this." She said as she showed him. "She should put one arm over yours, like this. Your hand should hold hers, like this." As she spoke she placed their arms and hands in the correct positions.

Masking his anxiety proved difficult, this wasn't something he had any real interest in, but the payoff would be worthwhile.

"Now, this dance requires hip movement, so you need to keep your knees bent, and when you step, you move with your hips. It goes slow, quick, quick, slow." She proceeded to show an example of the movement. "OK, now try."

It was a struggle, and the effort left him feeling awkward, but Cassidy was a natural.

"Alright. Let's try again." Jess approached his side, placed her hands on his shoulders. "Keep your upper body straight, your frame straight. Your eyes stay on your partner, you need to isolate your lower body from your upper body, focusing your movements to only your lower body. This time, in your mind, add the count in, one, two, three, four, to the movement." She gave another demonstration. "Go ahead, try again."

A few more tries with instructor intervention and he improved, but the awkwardness never left. How did Cassidy make it look so easy? At least his efforts to perfect the movements kept him distracted, because the way she moved was hot enough to set his blood on fire, and this was merely the basics. She smiled and her emerald green eyes sparkled.

The sound of a phone ringing upstairs broke through the low playing music.

"I'll let you two practice while I get that. I'll be right back." She hurried up the stairs.

"Thank you for this, Chase! You know, you're pretty good."

To hold back a scoff was impossible.

"You're only saying that because I'm not stepping on your feet." Her melodious giggle tickled his ears.

"Not true, though that is a bonus."

"Yeah, sure." He snickered. "By the way, how do you move your hips like that? You make it look way easier than it is."

"Humph. I can think of a few times you didn't have problems with hip movements."

He chuckled.

"That's different."

"No, it's not. You're just trading one dance for another." He pulled her to him.

"How about we test that theory later?"

Mischief played across her beautiful features. God, he was going to miss her.

"Sounds like a plan."

Approaching footsteps warned of Jess' return.

"Sorry about that. OK. Let's try to add the lady's underarm turn." They stopped as she drew near them. "I'm just going to borrow Chase here for a minute."

With that Cassidy backed away and observed. The momentary anxiety was assuaged when she appeared genuinely interested in what Jess intended to teach instead of reacting with a familiar jealous stance he was used to from women in previous relationships.

The lessons continued and Cassidy just flew through it all like a pro. It seemed she only needed to see the move to imitate them. At the end, his libido was more than eager to get out of there and back at the motel.

"That was fun." Cassidy exclaimed, wrapping her arms around him appreciatively when they reached the car.

Her eyes shone like polished gems. The way the moonlight played off her silken honey strands and creamy skin as a slight breeze blew by created a stunning vision, and he burned the image in his mind. He wanted to remember her this way for however long he would be gone, a stunning goddess to illuminate his darkest dreams.

"I'm glad you enjoyed yourself."

"Did you?"

"It was alright." Truth be told, he still didn't care for that kind of thing, but he'd tolerate it if he could see her this way again.

Her face beamed before shadows clouded those lovely green orbs.

"I hope we can do this again someday." The sadness in her tone clawed at his heart.

Never before had he so dreaded a mission, but he couldn't back out. Nothing killed him more than seeing her so disappointed and knowing he would miss out on ultrasounds and other important milestones ripped away his insides. Hopefully he'd be back before the child was born.

"We will, don't worry. When I get back, we can go do whatever you want. Now let's get back. As I recall, you wanted to show me how grateful you are." He couldn't help but quirk a grin.

She gave him a playful slap to the chest and her voice gave none of the bite her words might suggest.

"Oh, Chase, you're so awful!"

"You wait 'til we get back and I'll show you awful." He teased.

He wasted no time when they got back either. His mouth was on hers before they even got through the door. In the blink of an eye, clothes were strewn about the room, hands and mouths roamed each other's flesh as he worked to give her a night to remember. She was greedy for every rapturous moment, and when she couldn't go on and crashed from exhaustion hours later, he considered it mission accomplished.

The alarm startled him awake. He struggled to rouse from bed, fighting fatigue. There was no way to figure out how long he laid awake watching her sleep. She had the semblance of a sleeping angel and he wanted to get as much of her as possible. No way would he be sleeping on the plane either.

Cassidy's groan of protest toward the intrusive sound had him wanting to repeat the entire night before but he had to get ready. Leaning over, he shut off the annoying racket.

"How are you this morning?"

A frown adorned her lips.

"I think the same way as Juliet the morning Romeo left from banishment. I'm not sure how other women deal with these things."

His anxiety prickled.

"You are stronger than you realize, Cassidy. The strongest woman I know. If anyone can manage this, it's you."

"I'm going to miss you." It barely came out a whisper.

She was clearly fighting tears. She wasn't making this easy. His gut wrenched horribly.

"Let's go out to eat, then I can drive you to pick up your car right after. I need to stop somewhere before I go to the plane but you can meet me there a few minutes before one. Alright?" She nodded in agreement.

Time flew at lightning speed and there was no slowing it down. Before he knew it he stood at the foot of the stairs leading to the door of the plane, waiting. One o'clock came, and he clutched the small velvety box in his pocket with the grip of death.

Where was she? Did she get overwhelmed and scared off? Was she really standing him up?

"Come on! We gotta go man!"

"Wait a minute!" His blood seared beneath his flesh.

Of all people, he never thought she'd stand him up. Rage consumed him. He felt every bit the fool. She ran away, just like every time before. Five minutes after one.

"We're not waiting any longer! Let's go!"

Just as he turned to march up the stairs, the sound of a speeding car reached his ears, followed by the desperate pleading sound of Cassidy's voice.

"Chase!" Too little, too late, he was beyond done.

Chapter Twenty-Three

Cassidy

In a huff she rushed up the stairs to the entrance of the aircraft after practically jumping out of the still moving police cruiser. If not for the car crash, she would have been there. The incident had left her scratching her head. All those who desired to harm her got locked up, so why had the car pursued her?

The accident seemed unquestionably deliberate, and the driver got away. Her only luck had been escaping with only a few scratches, bumps, and bruises. That, and the officer that arrived had enough mercy to drive her to the airport after finding out where she was going and why. Once again, she found herself without a vehicle.

"Chase, wait!" Frustration emanated off him in waves.

He stopped, turned as she reached the top, his eyes stone cold.

"Look, Cassidy, this..." He pointed his finger alternately between them. "Is not working."

She sucked in a breath. Her chest constricted painfully.

"Wha - what do you mean?"

"After all this time, you say you love me, you said you'd be here for me, but you didn't show. After what I did for you, you don't care enough about me to see me off?"

"Chase? I wanted to, I tried, I was in an accident, I was lucky to get the officer to drive me here. Please don't be mad at me! I-..."

"Shut it! I don't want your excuses." Tears started down her cheeks.

"That's not an excuse, that's what happened!" Like the scratches on her face weren't enough, did he not know her enough to realize she wouldn't stand him up intentionally? "Let me make it up to you when you get back, a movie, comedy, anything!"

Did he not realize by now that even after how much he hurt her, she still loved him? She'd have helped him build an empire if possible. It was just her luck, the Powers-That-Be just had to intervene, and as always, it left her on the losing end. Between the two, surely misery was her destiny.

"I don't want anymore lies. You're nothing but a loser, waste of my time and energy, and I want nothing more to do with you. I can find a hundred women, a thousand, prettier, smarter, real winners, any of which to replace you. From now on, you're dead to me."

He spun around, opened the door.

"Chase, *please* listen! I tried! I..."

He elbowed her when she touched his arm, hard, causing her to lose her balance as he entered and slammed the door behind him. She fell backwards, down the steep set of stairs. Her breath caught in her lungs. Hands reaching out for anything, she grabbed the flimsy rail which snapped off. Searing pain filled her as the massive piece tore into her shoulder and down her chest, piercing her heart as she continued to fall, landing on the pavement.

A sizable jagged piece of black metal protruded from below her ribs. A crowd gathered like vultures eagerly waiting for the kill, and her vision went hazy. The sound of the plane engine became distant. She barely made out faces and panic stricken voices. To her dismay her body just wouldn't move, her arms and legs rebelled against every effort. One blurry face came close to hers, pulling something from his ears, and an eerie melody floated in the air, something about change. It was the last thing to infiltrate her ears before losing consciousness.

"Quickly, we need to operate! There's damage to the left ventricle, send her to..." She fell back into darkness.

Chase appeared before her, ocean-blue eyes menacing. He just stood there, amid total darkness, powerful, all encompassing, like the seductive form of Satan himself. Eve never would have stood a chance alone with him.

"Chase, I'm sorry! There's just some things beyond my control! I wanted to, I..."

"Don't waste your breath, I hate you. You mean nothing to me, never have, never will."

"Why would you say that?"

His laughter reflected his hatred.

"You're so stupid."

How could such horrid, hateful things come from such a beautiful package? It wasn't fair! Fire consumed her body, and she tensed, cried out in pain, moisture welling in her eyes.

"I love you, Chase! Why would you...?" He sneered.

"Because you're such a gullible idiot! I never loved you, but you ate it up." Laughter ensued.

Heartbreak and despair consumed her. Death beckoned her.

"Hold on, Cassidy! Stay with me!" She heard a familiar voice through the fog in her mind, but opening her eyes proved impossible.

Joe? Despite her best efforts her body remained immobile, darkness called her once again.

"We're losing her."

"No! Cassidy, fight! Do you hear me? You need to fight!"

Flames and dead bodies surrounded her, some place similar to the safe-house where she'd stayed with Chase, only the walls comprised of pure flame. The stench of death and scorched flesh overwhelmed her. Dead eyes of familiar, zombie-like faces stared into her accusingly, terror threatened to consume her. Was this hell?

Did Chase see these kinds of things when he slept? What nightmares did he have? But she couldn't be sleeping, the painful burning that scorched every inch of her flesh felt far too real. She screamed in agony once more before collapsing to her knees.

"Hi sweetheart." Chase's voice, the soft, rich, honeyed tone she remembered echoed in the distance.

Her heart skipped a beat.

Looking up, Chase's hardened eyes greeted her, and she swallowed.

Her heart bled. Why would he torture her like this?

"You were a nice little pet, such a pretty puppet." Her chest constricted.

"Stop! This isn't fair! You're... you're killing me!" He laughed.

"Oh come on. Don't pretend to be the victim, Cassidy. You're just being emotional. You shouldn't take everything so personally."

He reached into her chest, hand clutching her heart in a vice-like grip, and pulled.

She screamed in agony.

"Cassidy, come on! You *need* to fight!"

That familiar voice again, Joe. Still she remained motionless, her eyelids wouldn't budge.

"We've lost it."

"What do you mean?" Joe sounded frantic.

"Her injuries are too extensive, she's miscarrying."

"Oh my God! *WHAT*?"

"Oh no, we're losing her again!"

No!

The black void enveloped her once more.

She found herself once more in a world of darkness and fire. Wicked laughter surrounded her, Chase's.

"I never thought I'd meet someone so easy to string along." Scanning her surroundings proved useless, he was nowhere in sight. "You were so crazy for me, fell so hard for me, it couldn't have been any easier. Such a stupid woman hanging on to some stupid crush."

Just a crush? He dared reduce her feelings to a mere crush? A meaningless infatuation? Her eyes swelled with moisture.

Flames crept up her body, singing her flesh painfully, yet she continued searching for the source of the voice. She came to a dead end when she reached a pit, spanning as far and deep as the eye could see. Inside was a fiery fire, flames rising hotter than the area in which she tread. Was she imagining it, or were there screams coming from within?

She whirled around to see Chase, a dark aura surrounding him.

He was a powerful force, and she felt weak, helpless, while there he stood, infinitely more devastating than the demons that tormented her. Powerful enough to lift her to unbelievable heights, or send her to her ultimate destruction. The nearer he drew, the more she backed away as terror engulfed her. Upon reaching the ledge she peered down.

A pair of strong hands clutched her biceps.

"Oh sweetheart, you're here with me, I got you." The words sounded insincere, more like a mockery of the drive when she realized he was alive, and she turned to see him about an inch from her face, bearing a sinister grin, before he shoved her over.

Every cell erupted in a pain worse than anything she could imagine as the fire engulfed her, and only worsened, cresting in an explosion of agony as she screamed until her voice had gone.

Her eyes burst open, and she inhaled sharply, sending a fresh burst of pain to her chest. It took a moment to focus. Every part of her body hurt, burned.

"You're awake!"

She managed a weak smile.

"Yeah." Speaking proved difficult, her mouth was dry, and even the act of talking was painful.

Joe stared down at her, moisture in his eyes, leaning on the rail of the hospital bed.

"For a while I wasn't sure you'd make it. They resuscitated you from death at least twice. You had surgery to repair the damages to your heart, but it'll be a while before your sensory nerves stop flaring and you're healed up enough to leave. That thing they pulled out of you did some real damage. You're lucky you're not paralyzed, let alone dead."

"Lovely." She moved to sit up but Joe stopped her, sadness and pity written across his face.

"You need your rest. After everything your body's been through, and what you lost, you should really go easy on yourself."

She put her hand over her abdomen, looked down, noticed the angry scar spanning the length of her chest.

"Where's..."

"You lost the baby." Holding back the floodgates was impossible.

Given her condition, even if she hadn't suffered the injuries, there was a big chance she'd have lost it, but also a chance she'd have gone to term. Now she'd never know. Her body convulsed as she sobbed.

Did Chase know what happened? Would he care? Just thinking about what he'd said to her, she didn't believe so. Things he'd never said to her in all the years they'd known each other.

"I'm sorry for what you've been through." Joe murmured, petting her head, trying to offer what little comfort he could.

Another three weeks passed before they released her from the hospital. She stood before the dance club where Sheila and Joe waited inside, adjusting her floor length, low cut leather spaghetti strap dress which had a slit from hip to floor. After fixing her black lace mask and black wings for comfort, then checking that her black cherry lipstick was perfect, she stepped through the door.

Everyone's masquerade costumes were amazing, beautiful, but none were as dark as hers.

As Danzig's voice bled through the speakers, she searched for them, yet her mind wandered. She'd had enough of the pain, feeling beat down, the demons that haunted her. Her mind was at the same place as years ago not long after finding out Chase had joined the forces, rock bottom, longing for the drug induced numbness that helped her coast through life so long ago, but that would no longer suffice.

For so long the Powers-That-Be were needlessly cruel, though she never complained. What would be the point? Chase's hurtful words didn't help either. She was tired of kowtowing, always putting herself last and trying so hard to make everyone else happy at the expense of herself. Things were going to change, she was going to get what she wanted out of life, and to hell with everything else.

"Cassidy?" She turned to see her friend donning a deep purple medieval gown, a similar colored lace mask on her face which made her violet eyes pop.

"Hey, Sheila!"

"Wow! You look amazing! It's like you're a totally different person!"

The sense that someone was watching nagged at her. Probably nothing. With effort she shook it off. Not that it mattered. She didn't care anymore about if anyone tried anything. She lost the ability to care about almost everything.

The days of letting her heart get trampled on were over. It was past time to get the things she wanted. The old Cassidy was gone, and if anyone wanted to get in her way, they could go down in flames right along with her. A wicked grin crept upon her lips.

"Thank you, Sheila! So do you, and that's just what I was going for."

Chase and Cassidy's Playlist

Faded - Alan Walker

Team - Iggy Azalea

Rise - Katy Perry

I'll Be - Edwin McCain

Don't Kill The Magic - Magic

Awake - Godsmack

Don't Let Me Down - The Chainsmokers ft Daya

No Broken Hearts - Bebe Rexha

Bad Things - Machine Gun Kelly ft Camila Cabello

Feel Invincible - Skillet

Get Up - Korn ft Skrillex

Changes - Deftones

Under Her Black Wings - Danzig

www.ingramcontent.com/pod-product-compliance
Lightning Source LLC
Chambersburg PA
CBHW050743250626
47155CB00005B/1896